VENGEANCE
IS
MINE

VENGEANCE IS MINE

First edition. January 29, 2022.

ISBN: 979-8201261511

Written by J. H. Dehart.

Table of Contents

I dedicate this book to my mother Joyce Hostetler who gave me my passion for reading when I was a very little girl. She always had books in our home and made sure we visited the library often. Thanks, Mom, for the precious gift of reading and always being their to encourage me in my writing.

REVELATION

PROLOGUE

Iraq 2013

He gasped trying to catch his breath in the choking dust that swirled around him and his fellow marines. Struggling onto his hands and knees he shook his head trying to stop the ringing in his ears. The rumble of a large truck heading toward him made him frantically wave his arms trying to clear the air so he could see which way he should go.

Someone yelled, "Captain Sadler!"

"Over here!" he shouted back, standing up, and was relieved as he saw Private Benson walking through the clearing dust. Benson hurried to him and skidding to a halt asked, "Sir, are you ok?"

Captain Jon Sadler stood before the private brushing the dirt and debris from his hair as he glanced around trying to discover where his helmet had landed after the IED had detonated. He paused to answer the young man. "Yes, I'm fine. How is everyone else?"

Captain Sadler felt his stomach flip when Private Benson replied, "Private Murphy is dead, Sir." He waited, giving his captain a moment to digest this news and then continued, "Sergeant Austin has lost both legs and the chopper is on the way in to pick him up."

"Take me to him, Benson," Jon demanded, covering any feelings of regret or sadness behind a mask of strict discipline. He must be strong for his marines. They expected him to be a strong leader they could depend on. Benson turned and hurried toward the medic truck with Jon following right on his heels.

Jon walked calmly up to his injured marine and gently placed his hand on his shoulder. Sergeant Austin glanced up at him with pain-filled eyes. "Captain, I'm sorry," he whispered.

Jon felt his gut tighten. How could a man lying there with half of his body blown away be apologizing?

"Marine, you have served honorably and with courage." He stepped back and saluted his injured marine declaring, "Simper Fi!"

Jon felt concern wash over him when Sergeant Austin's eyes closed, and his head rolled sideways as Jon stepped away from his side when the medics rushed in to grab the stretcher; nearby the chopper was coming in for a landing. Jon turned and rushed away from the scene with deep regret over what had happened, he had long ago learned not to let anger cloud his judgment. Anger made one sloppy and prone to stupid mistakes. He made his way toward the surviving Hummer and instructed the driver to take him to HQ.

CHAPTER 1

Seattle

Spring 2025

Jon woke up in a cold sweat as the remnants of a nightmare started to fade. He had left the Marine Corp 10 years ago but often still had nightmares. He told no one. He was a marine. He could deal with this. Jon sat up on the side of his bed, running his hands through his short sandy blond hair, waiting until his beating heart slowed, then standing up, he stretched to his full 6ft. 2inch height, and headed for the bathroom, going to the sink. Splashing cold water in his face he gazed at his haggard reflection in the mirror, rubbing the sleep from his deep blue eyes, wondering if the nightmares would ever cease. Popping a couple aspirin in his mouth, hoping it would ease his headache, he stepped into the shower. Feeling better when he finished, he made his way toward the kitchen to grab a cup of coffee and a bite to eat, then stepped toward the floor to ceiling windows of his 40th floor penthouse with a commanding view of Elliot Bay. He watched the sky start to lighten with daybreak. The soft pastel pink shades of the sky reflecting on the still waters of the bay, as the activity on the street and wharfs below steadily begin to pick up; slowly he turned away from the scene before him. Today he must go into the office. He dreaded the requirement of his father that he must show up at the office at least twice a week.

He had planned on making the Marines his career, but fate had decided otherwise, causing him to leave the Corps when his father had been in a car accident leaving him severely disabled, fighting for his life. As the oldest son he felt obligated to step into his father's shoes and run the business, but it was so much more rewarding to be hiking in the mountains than fighting the concrete jungle. After dressing quickly in a business suit, Jon made his way to the parking garage and climbed into his Ferrari, hoping to beat the morning traffic and his father to work. He hated big cities. That was the reason his home in the city was on the 40th floor, away from the noise and the people. He quickly drove the couple miles to the high-rise office building. Slowing, he pulled into the company parking garage swinging the car into his private parking space and exiting the vehicle he grabbed his briefcase and made his way to the elevator. Today was worse than most days. They were having a meeting about new plans to expand the business into new foreign markets, and as CEO it was his duty to preside over the meeting.

He rushed to his office ignoring his secretary who said, "Good morning, Mr. Sadler" only to come face to face with his father. Amos Sadler! Founder and President. The name and the man could still send a sliver of fear creeping up his spine. His discomfort deepened when Amos Sadler turned his hard, grey eyes toward his son. What have I done now? Jon wondered. Amos Sadler was a giant of a man poured into an average sized body, driven and ruthless, not caring whom he ran over or destroyed in his pursuit of wealth. He had taken an idea to improve the speed and reliability of the internet and turned it into a multi-billion-dollar company called Prism Technologies.

Amos asked coldly, "You're aware we have a meeting this morning?"

Jon bit back an angry retort, replying calmly, "Yes, sir."

"Why are you late?"

Jon felt his ire rising as he fought to remain calm. "The meeting is not for three hours at 10a.m."

"I'm fully aware of what time the meeting is. You know I like to meet with you before the meeting to go over the particulars!"

Jon held his breath for a few seconds to quiet the angry outburst sitting on the edge of his tongue. Taking a deep breath, he said, "Let us begin." as he sat down at the conference table in his office, to confront the only man in the world who could make him lose his cool.

The meeting finally over, Jon made his way to his waiting car. Let his father get angry. He was leaving. The meeting had gone very well, and the deal had been sealed but Jon was feeling the weight of his responsibilities crushing down on him. His father could reach him on his phone if he needed to talk with him. He aimed the car for Interstate 90 and sped away toward his log home in the Cascade Mountains. His phone rang, interrupting his angry thoughts, and he groaned loudly when his father's number came up on the screen.

Slowing the car, he spoke into the Bluetooth. "Yes?"

His father demanded irritably, "Get back here. I was not through with you."

"On my way!" Jon snapped back and hung up on his father before he could say anything more. Today was turning into a really lousy day. What more could happen?

Jon once again stormed past his secretary heading to his father's office. Pausing at the door he took a few deep breaths to settle his raging anger, then knocked and entered when directed by his father. Amos Sadler sat at his desk mercilessly engineering events to follow his whims and wishes. Jon thought all he needed was a crown because he was definitely king of his domain. Jon waited quietly just inside the door for his father to finish. He was fully aware he was going to be made to wait as long as it took his father's anger to cool, so he was shocked when his father glanced up at him almost immediately saying, "Come in, Jonathan. We need to talk."

Whatever was on Amos' mind was serious when he called him Jonathan. The younger braced himself for the coming storm. "Come sit down," Amos demanded, waving him toward a chair in front of his desk.

When he was seated, Amos glanced at Jon and wasted no time getting to the point. "Are you aware the bunker is almost finished?"

Wow, that had come out of left field, thought Jon. "To tell the truth, Dad, I hadn't given it much thought lately."

"Well think about it now," He demanded. "I need you to go to Virginia and supervise the final completion."

Jon gazed at his father in stunned silence. Go check on the bunker? Excitement surged through him. He was being given a marvelous opportunity. The mountains of Virginia were not the mountains of the West Coast, but mountain wilderness was mountain wilderness wherever it was located.

Struggling to control his excitement he said calmly, "You know I'll make sure the job is finished to your requirements." Unable to contain his smile, he asked, "When do I leave?"

To his shocked surprise his father smiled back at him. "I'll give you an hour to get yourself packed, and in the meantime, I'll have the jet made ready for you," Amos paused and was rewarded with his son's astonished reaction to his next statement. "Son, enjoy yourself. Take a short hike along the Appalachian Trail."

Jon stood up and reached for his father's hand, shaking it briskly, saying, "Thanks, Dad!"

"Keep me updated." Amos Sadler demanded harshly, slipping back into his comfort zone, but Jon continued to smile at his dad as he left. Great! Today was turning into an amazing day after all!

Speeding back to the penthouse, he jumped from the car tossing the keys to the valet saying, "I'll be out of town for a few days, park her in the locked garage parking space."

"Yes, sir. Very good, sir. Have a safe trip."

Jon had turned away and didn't hear the valet as he rushed into the building heading toward his private elevator. In seconds he was at his penthouse.

He paused to call his mother. "Mom, I'm going out of town."

"Ok, honey."

"Dad will update you about what is going on. I'll call you when I have arrived."

"Stay safe and I love you, Jon."

"Love you, Mom."

He had wondered more than once how his sweet, devoted mother had ever seen any redeeming qualities in his father that made her want to marry him. He must have been very different 45 years ago.

CHAPTER 2

Jon settled into a seat on his father's private jet and felt the cares of his life temporarily slip from his shoulders when the plane lifted from the ground. Jon loved feeling the moment the wheels left the earth and he felt himself and the plane floating in the air. He loved flying! He watched the scenery pass by under the plane until darkness settled on the land, then he reclined in the seat and dozed. Within hours the pilot woke him announcing they would be landing at Roanoke Airport in Virginia in about 20 minutes. He pushed the footrest down and again gazed out the window. He saw tiny patches of lights shimmering in the black darkness from the small cities in the area; miniscule compared to Seattle. Even the city of Roanoke was a town compared to Seattle, but he liked the quaint city with its early 20th century high rises standing stately beside the tall modern gleaming towers nestled in the Shenandoah Valley, surrounded by the lush green Blue Ridge Mountains. The pace of life in this city was slow, not at all like a large metropolitan area. A city like this he could live in. As the plane came in for a landing, Jon finally saw the large lighted star which shone like a beacon, on the highest mountain peak in the city, welcoming him back to Roanoke. Once, the plane had landed, he was again surprised by the lack of activity and the calm, laid back atmosphere of the airport. It appeared that no plane had recently landed, or one was getting ready to take off, as he was the only passenger in the terminal. Several employees waved friendly greetings at him as he made his way to the car rental desk. The clerk at the desk was efficient and friendly, speaking to Jon with that slow mountain accent that he was beginning to like and understand. Maybe he should have a talk with his father about opening an office here and he could run things, instead of just using the excuse he was searching for real estate to open a business in Roanoke, to cover up the real reason he was here. He quickly found himself behind the wheel of his rental, headed to a local hotel. Nothing fancy, just some place to rest for the few hours until daybreak.

The next morning, he was up early and heading north on the Blue Ridge Parkway as the sun peeked over the horizon painting the sky fire red, splashed with bright orange. Jon was appropriately appreciative at the sight as he topped a mountain ridge and could gaze in all directions as far as he could see. When he had traveled about an hour, he exited the Parkway and turned onto a narrow two-lane road heading toward the Jefferson National Forrest. He knew the way well as he had been making this trip frequently over the last 10 years. After a few miles he was in an undeveloped, uninhabited part of the state. He was sure that many a person had headed down this road only to wonder why the road was here and turn around to head back the way they had come. After a couple miles he came to the eight foot tall fence with razor wire on top and large signs every 500feet which declared the land was government property and trespassers would be prosecuted. His father had left the fence and the signs up to deter nosey intruders when he had purchased the compound and the surrounding 500 acres.

Jon slowed as he drew close to the gate and using the remote control, he pushed the button opening the gate. Once inside the gate he closed it and continued on his way. As he made his way slowly along the narrow mountain dirt road, he admired the men who were driving those large trucks in and out of here delivering building supplies. He was yet again stunned when the small river came into view as it danced over the boulders heading down the mountain to the James River past the bunker toward which he was driving. The land leveled to a small even plain in the small holler in which the bunker stood with the mountains rising steeply on three sides, the trees growing thick and tall, blocked the morning sun. He was almost there.

The bunker was an abandoned communications building, which the American people were not aware they had built. It had been built to keep communications up and running in the event a catastrophe took out the regular phone lines or cell towers. It was built to withstand an EMP, a nuclear explosion, and had a ventilation system that would protect the inhabitants from chemical and biological attacks. The bunker had the equipment to produce its own electricity and pump its own water from a well. It was completely and brilliantly self-contained and would have comfortably housed ten people for about three months, who would have been locked in, if there had been an emergency. The ironic thing was that Jon's father had been one of many who had made the bunkers obsolete by the 1990's when they had made the internet and wireless phone service so efficient, that the government had shut them down. Now the communication bunkers were scattered from coast to coast in remote areas going to ruin.

Even though Jon thought his father was overreacting on his beliefs that the world was soon going to descend into anarchy and chaos, he was intrigued with the bunker. His father had purchased the bunker about 15 years ago and started serious renovations five years ago. The bunker had been mostly underground with a large communication tower that had towered above the mountain ridge top, which had been removed long ago and extensive landscaping had been done outside to make the bunker look as if it were a natural part of the mountain. Fill dirt, boulders and large trees had been trucked in and planted and he was always amazed at how the forest had taken over, completely hiding the bunker. If a person did not know the bunker was there, they could walk right past it without ever seeing it. The construction team had done an amazing job. He exited the car and walked up to the side of what appeared to be a small hill, pushing through the thick undergrowth until he came to what looked like the side of the mountain. He pushed back a grass covered flap and entering the code into the control panel, he watched the hidden door begin to quietly slide open, revealing an inner steel door which was also sliding open. He was thrilled to see a man standing guard with an assault rifle pointed at him when the door slid open, and he stepped into a tunnel which would lead him to the main bunker.

"Great job." Jon told the man.

He replied, "Glad to see you, Mr. Sadler. We were informed you would be arriving today. Mr. Akers is waiting for you in the main living area."

"Thank you," Jon said walking past him down the hall to enter the living area. He was always amazed at the transformation. When he had first investigated the bunker with his father, they had entered a 5,000 square foot rectangular room with 15foot high ceilings. There was a lower level which housed the generators, air filtration, sanitation systems, pumps and storage containers for the well water. The total floor space was 10,000 square feet. His father had the construction crew construct the large main living area with a family room and a full-service kitchen and build two hallways off the main living area which contained a bathroom at the end of each hall and four large bedrooms on each hall. A third hallway which was the family's private hall contained five extra-large bedrooms with a large bathroom in his parent's room and another at the end of the hall. There was a longer fourth hallway which led down toward the back of the lower level in which his father had had them construct a four-stall stable and a secure back entrance.

Jon walked up to Mr. Akers, the construction foreman, reached forward to shake his hand saying, "Hello, Fred. Looking great. Can we go on a tour?"

"Yes, sir, Mr. Sadler."

Jon asked Fred, "Is the electricity working?"

"Yep." The foreman replied, with a smile, flipping a switch, flooding the room with bright light.

"I would like to see the propane tanks which have been installed since I was last here."

"This way, sir." The tall thin man turned to lead Jon out of the back entrance. Two 30,000 gallon industrial size propane tanks stood ready to be filled. The room in which they were housed had been constructed underground next to the bunker. Everything was clean and tidy. Jon was pleased. Next, they toured the lower floor and the stable, then returned upstairs and toured the hallways, bathrooms and bedrooms. Jon was pleased with the built-in bunkbeds and dresser/entertainment center in each room on the visitor hallways and the well-furnished family rooms. When they returned to the kitchen Jon examined the kitchen and appliances.

Jon smiled. "I'm very pleased Fred, everything looks great. I'll be staying here for the next few days until after the propane is delivered and the equipment tested."

"Yes, sir." Fred replied and turned to go check on the progress of the construction crew who were connecting the propane lines to the equipment while Jon began a serious inspection of the construction on the upper floor.

Two days later the propane had been delivered and once again Jon was in awe of the drivers of those big rigs that maneuvered down the narrow road to the bunker.

CHAPTER 3

Jon packed supplies for an overnight trip into the Appalachian Highlands and informed Fred of his plans, then drove to a private hostel at one of the many entrances to the Appalachian Trail and told them his plans, asking if he could leave his car parked in their parking lot. They were as friendly as everyone else he had met in these mountains and gave him permission to park his car. After parking the car, he set off on his two-day hike.

He hiked five miles before he came to the Trail marked by the familiar white paint mark on a tree trunk. He set off hiking north. The trees had just begun to bud, and most were covered in tiny pale green leaves. He had picked this time for his hike because the weather was forecast to be warm and dry, and he was not disappointed. Before long he paused at one of the many points on the trail where he could look across the sweeping vista at the rolling mountains and valleys dotted with farms and tiny towns stretching to the horizon. He knew that approximately 350 miles to the east was the Norfolk Naval Shipyard where he had spent most of his Marine Corps career. Maybe on his next trip east he would try to head that way for a visit. He hiked until the sun was sinking low in the sky enjoying the forest as numerous birds sang, enjoying the warm spring day as much as he was. He found a level spot just off the Trail and quickly had his one-man tent erected. He ate the prepackaged meal he had brought with him deciding not to start a fire, keeping his bear spray near, and his pistol strapped to his hip. It was rare but not impossible to be attacked by a bear, coyote, or other wildlife this deep in the forest. He sat outside as the sky grew inky black and with delight watched the stars begin to glow. He was thrilled it was a crystal, clear night and the sky was filled with a band of wispy looking cloud like images filled with stars cutting a path across the night sky. The Milky Way. Couldn't see this in the city he mused. He gazed at the expanse of twinkling stars and wondered, as he had on several occasions, if maybe there was a God. When he was out here in the wilderness alone, he could almost believe in God, but he convinced himself that if there was a God how could the world be in the shape it was in. Sighing he crawled into his tent and wrapped his sleeping bag around himself as the cool mountain air started to settle on the land once the sun had disappeared.

The next morning, he was up early to start his hike back to his car glad he had thought to bring a jacket as the morning was briskly cool. He made it back to the hostel where his car was parked at about lunchtime and went inside to grab a bite to eat. The food was nothing fancy. Just good hearty stick to your ribs fare that he ate with relish. Yep, he had decided to talk with his father about opening an office in Roanoke.

He returned to the bunker and called the pilot telling him he was flying back to Seattle tomorrow at 8a.m. He made one last round of the bunker, rechecking the newly installed and filled propane tanks, finding no leaks. The storage room was packed with many large black buckets of survival food and Jon knew when the construction crews had finished, he would pack the remaining shelves with ammunition and other necessary weapons. He was pleased to see the remaining furniture had been delivered and was stacked in a corner waiting for his mother to decorate. Everything seemed to be in order. He asked Fred to call the construction crew into the main living area for a meeting.

Once the men were assembled, he began. "I'm very pleased with the job you've all done. The bunker looks great." He paused while he handed each man a sealed envelope. "I've enclosed a bonus check for each of you. I'm buying your silence."

He smiled when the men chuckled and declared in unison. "You have it, Mr. Sadler."

He continued. "I really want to say you all have done an amazing job with the bunker and I just wanted to give you a special 'thank you' bonus. I'm leaving instructions with Fred about how I want things to be finished and I'm serious about your silence. I do not want any of you to talk about this project. Each of you were picked for your commitment to the company and to my father. If you ever need anything you know where to reach me. Good night, and I do hope we can work together again."

He headed to his room after he had bid Fred good-bye for the day, telling him he was leaving at daybreak in the morning. About 30 minutes after Fred had left for home, he came rushing back into the bunker causing Jon concern because he was so short of breath.

Jon asked, "Fred, are you ok?"

Fred stammered, "Mr. Sadler sir, there must be some mistake!"

"What's wrong, Fred?"

Fred started to shake the envelope Jon had just given him in the air between them. "This, Mr. Sadler. This is a mistake and I wanted to bring it to your attention, sir."

Again, Jon asked, "What's wrong, Fred?" as a glimmer of amusement, over Fred's anxiety, was making it hard for Jon not to grin widely at him.

Fred gulped and rushed on. "Are you aware, sir, of the amount written on this check?"

Jon finally grinned. "Yes, I am Fred. I told you I was very pleased with the job you did."

"But...but, Mr. Sadler, it's $500,000 dollars!"

Jon believed a job well done should be properly compensated and he had been serious about buying their silence. He knew the construction crew would be loyal to him and his family, and to Jon that was worth the three million he had paid to the crew in bonuses. His father could afford it.

"Fred, there is no mistake. I paid you exactly what I feel you deserved. If you need any help depositing the check just let me know and I'll give any help you need."

Jon was pleasantly surprised when Fred grabbed his hand and started shaking it briskly. "Thank you, Mr. Sadler! Thank you very much." Fred pumped Jon's hand up and down as he started to visibly shake and mumbled, "I give you my word the work will be finished to your satisfaction."

Jon continued smiling, enjoying the feelings induced by giving so much joy. "I know you'll finish the job, Fred. I guess I'll tell you good night again because I need to get packed and ready for my flight early in the morning."

"Yes, sir. Good night, sir," Fred stammered.

"And, Fred?"

"Yes sir, Mr. Sadler?"

"Take the family on a vacation."

Fred finally smiled. "Yes, I will. Thank you and have a safe trip."

Turning, he walked out of the bunker. Jon wished he could see the reactions of all the men and their families when they realized how much the checks were for, he had paid the rest of the crew $200,000 each. It was a new and wonderful feeling to be spreading such happiness. He would have to do this more often.

CHAPTER 4

The next morning, Jon made it to the airport without incident and this time the airport was buzzing with activity as one plane was getting ready to leave and two had just landed. He made his way toward the entrance for the private jets; finding the pilot, they quickly cleared security and were given permission to take off. Within hours they were landing at SEA TAC. It was a typical Seattle spring day, with clouds hanging low, and mist dripping from every surface. Glancing at his watch Jon realized he still had time to check in with his father. He had called ahead and one of his father's limos was waiting for him. Crawling inside he instructed the driver to take him to the office. After being dropped off at the company officer's private entrance and riding the private elevator to the top floor, he knocked on his father's office door and was pleased to hear his father was still here when he bid him enter.

Jon entered and stood by the closed door waiting for his father to acknowledge him. He would not move until given permission. As he stood waiting, his mind wandered back to Marine Corp basic training when he had come to realize his father had prepared him well to follow and give orders. He had excelled. His younger brother Reggie (Reginald Xavier Sadler... Jon was glad he had not been the one saddled with that name) was a free spirit, encouraged and allowed to go his own way. Jon could not resent or be jealous of his 17 year old brother because he knew what drove his parents. Jon had only been five years old when his older brother Christopher had been diagnosed with leukemia. Jon only retained shadow memories of him. When Christopher was eight years old, just two weeks after they had discovered the vicious disease, he was gone, and his parents had sunk into a despair, leaving very little time for Jon and his baby sister Chloe. Amos Sadler had buried himself in his work, becoming a driven man and making billions in the process. He was one of the richest men in the world but that didn't bring him peace or happiness, thought Jon. Five years after Christopher had passed, they were blessed with another girl. Katherine...Katie to those who loved her. Life had settled into a forced happiness, his father working his life away, while his mother Betty poured herself into raising her children. When Jon was thirteen, his father had packed him off to a military academy when he had started to rebel against his father's iron rule. His father's strict ruthless demand for complete compliance and discipline had made military school a perfect fit. Jon had thrived. When he had graduated at seventeen, he had entered the Marine Corp immediately and was shocked when he learned a little brother was on the way. Reggie was six years old before Jon met him and was uncomfortable with the hero worship the young boy felt toward him, but an intense love blossomed for his little brother that surprised Jon. He catered to Reggie just like the rest of the family and was amazed that even though Reggie was spoiled, he managed to maintain a kindness and gentleness he had inherited from their mother.

Amos Sadler repeated himself, demanding sternly, "Jon! Did you hear me?"

Jon shook the cobwebs of memories clear and answered his father. "I'm sorry, sir. I'm tired."

Amos gazed at his son a few seconds, feeling a slight pinch of fear, wondering about the declaration he was tired, then rushed forward with his question. "So, how did you find things?"

"In excellent shape. Everything has been completed and inspected. The bunker is ready except for where Mom wants some furniture to be placed."

"Very good," Amos declared as he stood up. "Come home with me tonight for supper. Your mother wants to see you."

Disappointment settled on Jon. He really wanted to go home but agreed to go with his father. They both entered his father's limo and began the quiet journey to the family estate. When they arrived and walked through the main entrance Jon was delighted to see Chloe's small twin girls running to greet him with Reggie following close behind, Jon realized he was getting taller, and it wouldn't be long before he was as tall as Jon. Reggie glanced at him with eyes the same soft blue as their mother's and smiled. Jon grabbed the twins, surprised when he wrapped an arm around each girl and proceeded to twirl them. He wouldn't be able to do this for much longer as they were getting too big.

Putting the girls back on their feet he hugged Chloe and ruffled Reggie's blond hair as he slapped him on the back declaring, "Hey, little bro!"

Before the shenanigans could get out of hand, Amos Sadler strode into the room, and everyone quieted instantly. Jon hugged his petite, precious mother. Her soft grey hair perfectly coiffed, waved about her head while her soft blue eyes gazed at him with unconditional love. Next, he glanced at his sisters, Chloe tall and fashion model thin had their mother's wheat blond hair and soft blue eyes while petite Katie's hair was a soft chestnut like their father's, her eyes a softer grey than Amos' eyes.

Jon hugged Katie, then Chloe, asking, "Where's Jim?"

"On his way home from Houston," Chloe answered.

Amos watched his oldest children, proud of the adults they had become, but not knowing how to tell them. He looked at Betty asking, "Is supper ready?"

"Yes," she replied gently and reaching for his hand they walked together toward the dining room.

Their children and granddaughters followed silently, taking their seats when they reached the table. When everyone had their plate in front of them Jon was surprised when one of the twins asked, "Ain't we supposed to pray?"

Chloe smiled sheepishly when all eyes turned toward her. "Jim has been going to church."

Betty asked, "Church? When did this start?"

Chloe swallowed hard and plunged ahead, "Jim's brother got saved a few months ago and Jim has been going to church with him."

"Saved from what?" Amos demanded.

She paused, glancing at Jon. He was her older brother and had always helped her when their father questioned her. She loved her father but was more than a little afraid of him. For once however Jon shrugged.

Chloe answered honestly, "I'm not really sure, Daddy. I think from his sins."

"Sins? He doesn't seem to me to be such a terrible sinner he needs saving." Amos growled.

"I'm not sure I understand Daddy."

"I'll talk to him myself," declared Amos to Chloe's relief.

The family let the twins pray and ate their dinner in a strained silence which was highly unusual, because for all his demanding control, it always amazed Jon that Amos allowed his family to talk and socialize so much at the dinner table. Maybe this was what his mother saw in their father. Maybe before life had dealt harshly with him, Amos Sadler had been a kind, caring man. Jon doubted he would ever completely understand his parents. Supper was over more quickly than usual, and Jon excused himself asking if the chauffeur could return him home. He hugged his family and left.

CHAPTER 5

The following morning dawned sunny and clear, which was quite unusual for this time of year, Jon thought, standing near the living room windows gazing out across the Bay. After the week away, he was looking forward to going into the office and talking with his father about his ideas for opening an office in Roanoke. Suddenly the floor under his feet swayed briefly as a strange feeling washed over him. He had been through too many earthquakes to be concerned about this little quiver, but he couldn't explain the feeling of dread. Without warning, to his horror, a large passenger airline jet filled his field of vision as it dove straight for impact with the waters of Elliot Bay. He couldn't seem to pull his eyes away from the scene unfolding before his eyes, standing transfixed, gazing in disbelief and shock, as the plane flew into the water exploding upon impact sending a large section of the plane hurtling toward the Ferris wheel. Jon watched in stunned silence as the Ferris wheel was cut in half sending several of the gondola seats flying in several directions as debris was flung all over the bay and wharf, igniting multiple fires as the shrapnel tore through ships at anchor, warehouses and high-rise buildings. He finally glanced down at the streets below and was dismayed to see a tangle of vehicle accidents on the streets near the waterfront. He rushed to his bedroom and grabbing the phone dialed his mother.

He felt relief when he heard her worried voice. "Is this you, Jon?"

"Yes, Mom."

"What's happening, Jon? The news is saying hundreds of thousands of people have disappeared." She paused briefly and rushed on, fear causing her voice to tremble. "Jon... Jim and the twins have vanished."

Jon felt unimaginable despair flow through him. "What do you mean they have vanished?" he said a tad harshly.

He could hear his mother's tears. "I don't know, Jon. Chloe says they are gone."

"Where is Dad?"

"He went into the office early this morning."

"I'm going to go see him. Is Chloe with you? How about Reggie?"

"Yes."

"Good. Call Katie and tell her to come over and all of you stay at the house and keep the gates and doors locked. I'm not sure what's going on." He paused, "I'll call you from the office. I'm going to get Dad. Gotta, go Mom."

"Please be careful Jon."

"I will, Mom."

Jon threw on the first shirt and pair of jeans he grabbed and locking the door of his penthouse, started the long trek down 40 flights of stairs as the power had gone out when the plane crashed, leaving the elevator inoperable. He was glad when he reached the first floor, that he had been going down the stairs. Pausing to catch his breath, he exited the building to enter a world of utter chaos. Sirens and car alarms were blaring as thick black smoke roiled heavenward from the fires burning along the wharf. The few people he saw were walking around in a daze. Where was everyone? Was this another 9/11 and everyone was hiding or maybe everyone had vanished but a handful of people. Jon turned left and started the two mile jog to the office. With all the destruction, he knew it would be quicker to jog than drive. In fifteen minutes he was there and thrilled that the generators had turned on and he could ride the elevator to his father's office, which he entered without knocking. Amos Sadler swung away from gazing out of the window anger glaring in his eyes. Jon was surprised to see relief pass over his face when he saw him.

Jon wasn't here to argue with his father. "Come on, Dad. We need to get to the first floor, now."

Amos snapped, "What are you talking about?"

"A plane crashed near the wharf setting fires and destroying things. It'll take a while to get things fixed, and the power restored. The generator will only run for a few hours, and you cannot walk down 25 stories. Dad, you need to leave now while the elevator is still working."

Amos glared at Jon, then sighed. "Ok, son." Jon wished his father had snapped at him.

"Before we leave take a few minutes and watch this," his father said turning on the TV.

The local news anchor was visibly shaken as she updated the audience on the catastrophe unfolding. It appeared whatever was going on was worldwide. People had disappeared, planes and vehicles crashed, and power was out to most of the world.

Jon watched and listened for a few more minutes, then picked up the phone and turning on the building intercom he declared, "This is Jon Sadler, CEO. This is not a drill. We are in a state of emergency. You are ordered to evacuate the building immediately for your own safety. The building will be closed and locked until further notice. Please exit calmly and evacuate now! You will each be notified when to return to work."

"Come on, Dad, let's go. I'm taking you home to Mom."

Jon waited patiently as his father reached for his cane and walked slowly toward the door. When the 18-wheeler had run over the car his father had been driving 10 years ago, it had left him alive but critically injured. The whole left side of his body was twisted and deformed. He could barely use his left leg and the damage to his spine had left him permanently bent over. It was hard to believe looking at him now, he had stood 6 feet tall and was at the height of physical fitness when the accident happened. The accident had left him even angrier over the events in his life, but he was too stubborn to die or remain in a wheelchair, so he struggled walking with a cane.

When they reached the first floor Jon made his way to the security office finding Captain Gregory, who stood up when Jon entered the office, "Captain Gregory, I'm sure you heard what I said over the intercom."

"Yes, Mr. Sadler. I have my men doing a floor-by-floor search at this time to assure all employees have vacated the building. I'll personally see to it that the building is locked and secure."

"Thank you. I'll give you a call when the power has been restored and it is safe to return to work. Go home and take care of your family."

"Yes sir."

Jon rushed from the office to find his father talking to the receptionist at the main entrance. She was visibly shaken. Jon walked up to them saying gently, "Mrs. Kennedy, you need to go home to your family, security will be locking the building shortly."

She glanced at Jon, tears shimmering in her eyes, "I'm so afraid, Mr. Sadler. What's happening?"

"I don't know. Will you be ok getting home?"

"Yes, my son is almost here to take me home."

"Good. You will be called when it is safe to return to work. Come. We'll walk out with you."

They left the building to find Mrs. Kennedy's son waiting for her, along with Amos Sadler's limo. Saying goodbye, they made their way to the car.

Once inside the limo, which Jon was driving, because he had sent the chauffer home to his family, he called his mother. "Mom, Dad and I are on our way home." Then he handed the phone to his father.

He ignored what was being discussed between his parents, concentrating on driving home. He steered clear of the Interstate, using roads which wound through the many suburbs around Seattle, amazed to see the total chaos even here. No planes had crashed here, but many cars had, and several people were running around screaming for loved ones who were missing. One man stepped in front of the limo threatening Jon as he screamed and cursed at them. Jon pulled his pistol from the holster he had tucked under his left arm and silently pointed it at the man. The man stopped screaming and stood there glaring at Jon.

"Move!" Jon demanded loudly enough for the man to hear. "Move or I'll shoot you!"

Jon ignored his father in the backseat demanding him to stop threatening the man and continued to silently point the gun at the man's chest. The man finally shrugged his shoulders and moved aside barely getting out of Jon's way as he sped past him.

Amos continued to rant. "What's wrong with you, boy? This is not Iraq!"

Jon replied calmly, causing his father's concern to increase. "I know, Dad, but I have a feeling it's going to be much worse than Iraq ever was."

"Why do you say that, Jon?"

"I don't know, Dad, it's just a feeling. Whatever is happening around the world is something very extraordinary. The people disappearing, the earthquakes, the devastation around the world. Something isn't right."

Amos sat quietly for the rest of the ride home contemplating what Jon had said.

CHAPTER 6

In about 20 minutes they were home, pulling into the driveway. Jon pleased to see a security guard at the main gate, slowed, lowering the window. "Hello, Rodgers. Isn't today your day off?"

"Yes sir, Mr. Sadler. Captain Jenkins has called all security staff to report for duty to guard the estate until we can determine what's going on."

"Excellent! But what about your families?"

"Captain Jenkins told us to bring our families and we are all staying in the staff rooms above the garage."

"Thank you, Rodgers," Jon replied raising the window and drove to the front entrance.

As his father exited the limo, Jon said, "Dad, I'm going to find Captain Jenkins and I'll be in shortly."

After parking the car Jon went in search of Captain Jenkins, finding him in the security office. "Hello, Jenkins. I need to talk with you."

Captain Jenkins stood up. "Yes sir, how can I help you?"

"How many security people and their families are staying here?"

"Twenty guards, eight spouses and two teenagers, sir."

"Where are the children staying?"

Captain Jenkins said with despair. "They have all disappeared."

Jon asked, "All of them?"

The security guard nodded his head as Jon continued, "I'm sorry Jenkins. Tell the married men and their wives they can stay at the guest house for as long as needed, while the rest of the men can stay in the rooms above the garage." The guest house was a large, six bedroom home reserved for special guests whom his father wanted to suitably impress, situated near the swimming pool and the rooms above the garage had been built to house any staff that for whatever reason could not make it home after their shift.

"Thank you, Mr. Sadler. I'll let the others know of the changes."

"I'm going up to the house. Call if you need me."

Jon entered the mansion through the large sliding glass doors into the solarium and found his family sitting in the media room watching the news on TV. When he entered, Chloe ran to him, throwing her arms around his waist, and clinging to him desperately; sobbed.

Jon wrapped his arms around her holding her tightly as she blubbered, "They are gone Jon. Gone. All of them. We were having breakfast together when suddenly I was alone." She glanced up at the brother who had always taken care of her and made everything right. "What's happening, Jon?"

For the first time in his life Jon felt completely incompetent. He didn't have any answers. "I don't know but I'll find out," he promised.

Letting her go, he went to sit next to his mother. Everyone's eyes swung toward Reggie who declared, "I think I know what happened."

Before their father had a chance to bark at Reggie, Jon encouraged him. "Tell us what you think Reggie."

"Well, Jim had been talking to me after he got saved and he told me about this event that Christians call the Rapture and I think that is what happened."

Jon was curious. "What about this Rapture?"

Amos Sadler was glaring at his youngest child while the rest of the family gazed at him expectantly; Reggie continued, "Well, I don't know much but I do know he told me that when the Rapture happened all Christians would suddenly disappear and all the babies and little children too."

Amos roared, "Nonsense! All of that is nonsense!"

Jon thought it sounded farfetched, but no more ridiculous than aliens abducting people and personally he liked the thought of God taking certain people to heaven better than aliens taking people. "I don't know, Dad...it might be what happened. It's worth looking at all options."

"It's foolishness!" Amos declared. "I don't want to hear any more talk about it. I want to watch the news."

So, everyone sat in silence and watched in disbelief what was happening around the world. In addition to approximately several hundred million people disappearing, it was like hurricanes, earthquakes, tornadoes, tsunamis and wildfires had exploded all over the world at once, causing catastrophic damage and airplane, train, and vehicle wrecks around the world. It was terrifying!

Betty stood up saying, "I can't take anymore." Fleeing from the room. Chloe, Katie and Reggie followed her into the kitchen.

Reggie sat on a stool at the kitchen island while the girls helped Betty fix lunch. Carlitta, their housekeeper, came rushing into the kitchen saying frantically, "Oh my, Mrs. Sadler! I'm so sorry I was not here. I'll make your lunch."

Betty smiled. "I know you would Carlitta but I'm so upset about what is going on I needed to do something. We both can finish." The two women quickly had lunch prepared and Betty invited Carlitta to join them, but she had a firm belief against mingling with her employer and politely declined, rushing to finish her chores.

Chloe asked Reggie, "What did Jim say about the Rapture?"

Reggie felt overwhelmed because he had thought Jim was talking crazy and only half paid attention to him. "Chloe, I'm sorry but I didn't really pay attention to him. He told me that the world was very close to an event called the Rapture happening and when it did happen Jesus was going to take all born-again Christians, children and babies to heaven." He paused glancing toward his mother.

Betty said softly, "Go on, Reggie. You can tell us what he told you."

"He said that when it happened the world was going to become a very evil place."

Betty stopped what she was doing and glanced at her children, dread settling on her, "What did he mean Reggie?"

"I don't know, Mom." He glanced at his sister. "I'm sorry, Chloe, I thought he was crazy."

Chloe smiled. "It's ok, Reggie. I was thinking he was having mental issues too."

Reggie smiled at his sister and voiced an idea. "I'm going to get online and see what I can learn about the Rapture." He jumped from the stool and jogged out of the kitchen heading to his bedroom.

He spent the next couple hours researching the Rapture and he became more and more afraid. If what he was reading was true, they were in trouble. He realized the bunker was probably going to save their lives.

He also read what Jim had been telling him about being born again and accepting Jesus as his Savior. He had not told his family that he was starting to believe what Jim had been telling him and the more he read the more he felt the need to accept God's gift of salvation. He quietly prayed the prayer he had read in the article he was reading and felt relief he had finally listened to his heart. Standing up he decided to go in search of Chloe.

He found her near the pool crying quietly. He gently touched her shoulder and she glanced up at him. He sat down beside her asking, "Can I talk to you, Chloe?"

She wiped the tears from her eyes with her hands and blew her nose. "Sure, Reggie."

He swallowed and plunged ahead. "I was reading about the Rapture and started reading about that salvation Jim was talking about."

Chloe encouraged Reggie to continue. "I think what Jim was telling us was true and that is what happened, and Jim and the twins are in heaven."

He glanced away fearing her reaction, so was surprised when she said, "Yes, I believe you are right." She paused, then hurried on. "Please don't tell Mom or Dad, but when they disappeared, I was so afraid and upset because I realized Jim had been telling me the truth and I missed the Rapture. I begged God to save me and take me to heaven too, but I'm still here," she said with despair as tears started to slide down her cheeks again. Reggie placed his arm around her shoulders hugging her while she cried.

"Why doesn't God Rapture us now?" she managed to whisper.

Reggie's heart was breaking for his sister, but he didn't know how to comfort her and knowing his next words would cause more pain, he knew they still had to be said.

"Jim begged me to accept Jesus as Savior telling me that the Rapture was close to happening and if I wasn't saved I would get left behind and miss my chance to be raptured." Pausing briefly, gathering courage, he whispered in agony. "The Rapture was a one-time event, Chloe."

Chloe jumped up, running away from him, sobbing loudly. Reggie let her go. There was nothing he could do to ease her heartbreak.

Reggie sat alone by the pool wondering what he should do now he was saved. He had so many questions and knew of no one to help him. He would have to rely on the internet. Abruptly his quiet time of reflection was shattered by his irritated father yelling. Reggie knew his father was a driven man but managed to discern his anger was hiding tremendous heartache and bitterness. In spite of how hard his father tried to hide his feelings behind his domineering ways, Reggie knew he was loved.

Amos was saying as he stormed through the patio doors. "Reggie, what have you done to Chloe?"

Reggie moaned, "She was talking about Jim and the twins and became upset."

Reggie was surprised to see the bluster leave his father and his shoulders slump making him appear more shriveled as he walked toward Reggie and sat down beside him. Reggie didn't know what to say as this had never happened before, so he sat quietly waiting to see what would happen.

Nothing happened. His father sat beside him silently gazing at the pool. When Reggie could stand the strained silence no longer, he asked, "Dad, what are we going to do?"

Amos Sadler glanced at his youngest child and felt his heart constrict with a love so intense it frightened him. Amos fiercely loved all his children and knowing it was wrong to have a favorite, he couldn't help himself. Reggie was so much like his precious Betty, that the boy held a special place in his heart.

He answered honestly, "I'm not sure, Reggie. Tomorrow I hope to go into the office to assess what is going on around the world and here in Seattle." He paused and smiled a rare smile. "I have people I can talk to."

Reggie chuckled. "Can I go with you when you go to the office?"

This thrilled Amos. "Yes, of course you can!"

Unknown to them both Jon stood in the shadows watching them, feeling regret and happiness. Regret he did not know how to relate to their father, and happiness Reggie could have a conversation with him. He quickly turned and walked away when they both stood up and started for the house.

CHAPTER 7

The next morning Reggie was waiting with barely controlled excitement at finally being allowed to go to the office with his father and Jon. His hero worship of his older brother only grew stronger the older he became.

Jon was enjoying the constant questioning by Reggie as they drove into Seattle and was surprised to realize the boy was highly intelligent and how much he knew about the company. Once he glanced back at his father and brother, amused to see his father engaged in animated conversation with Reggie.

Jon noticed the vehicles in front of him slowing and wondered what was happening now. When he finally reached the roadblock and was signaled to roll down his window by the State Trooper waiting to talk to him, they had quieted in the back seat.

The Trooper asked, "Sir, what business do you have in Seattle?"

Jon answered respectfully, offering his driver's license to the officer for inspection. "Officer, I'm Jon Sadler, CEO of Prism Technologies and I'm taking my father to the office to see if we can find out what is going on."

The Trooper glanced at Jon's license, then bent down to glance into the back of the limo and standing back up, handed Jon his license, saying, "OK, you can go ahead but be careful. It's not safe in Seattle at this time."

Jon raised the window, after thanking the State Trooper, saying, "I wonder what has happened that Seattle is not safe?"

Amos replied, "Probably idiots rioting."

Jon did not reply. Neither did Reggie. Jon had a feeling his father was going to have to change his attitude or he might get seriously hurt or even killed.

Within minutes they had crossed Lake Washington and entered Seattle, Jon noticing black smoke still rising around the city. He was confused. He thought the fire department would have the fires out by now. Exiting from the interstate they entered the downtown area about six blocks from the office, into a full-blown nightmare. Jon drove slowly and carefully around the debris littering the streets and sidewalks. Burned furniture, and cars were strewn everywhere. The glass in the buildings was broken and some buildings had burned down leaving piles of smoldering rubble. Then the big shock was when they drove past five bodies lying next to each other as if they had been executed.

Amos declared, fear making his voice quiver, "Jon, don't stop. Take us straight to the office."

Jon had no intentions of stopping even though it seemed the city was abandoned. Jon knew better. The people who had engaged in the riots were home resting to be ready for round two tonight. Jon was glad to see the rioting had not spread near the office building and within minutes they arrived, Jon parking the limo in the secure stall in the parking garage, locking the car out of sight. They entered the building, Jon telling them both to wait near the private elevator as he went to inspect things. He was thrilled there was no evidence of any break-ins. He did a quick inspection of the first floor and finding no issues made his way to the control room and turned on the back-up power so the elevator would work. He turned off all lights inside and outside the building except the top floor. He checked the fuel supply and was pleased to see that only about ¼ of the fuel had been used since yesterday. Satisfied all was safe he made his way back to his father and brother. They rode silently up to the 25ᵗʰ floor.

Reggie was in awe. The building was more than he had imagined, being sleek and modern with steel and glass everywhere. He was finally here. He asked if he could do some research on a computer and again Amos was thrilled as he demanded of Jon, "Show him the computer room."

Jon smiled at the excitement in Reggie's eyes, saying, "Come on, little brother. I'll give you the grand tour." And they turned leaving Amos to his research.

After Jon had finished his guided tour for Reggie, he set him up at his desk on his own private company computer and told him to have fun. Today he had learned Reggie had inherited their father's genius. Before today Jon would've thought he was like any other 17 year old and was wasting his time playing worthless games on the computer, but he had learned Reggie didn't waste his time on frivolous games. Jon returned to his father's office to see if he needed any help.

Jon knocked on his father's office door and for once was glad when his father yelled irritably, "Come in."

Amos cast an angry glance at Jon. "What do you want?"

Jon smiled at his father, surprising Amos. "Nothing, Dad. Just wondering if I could help you with anything, before I go to the control room to run a systems check."

Amos' anger floundered and he replied quietly, "Everything is fine."

Jon turned to go, stopping to tell Reggie where he would be, and then took the elevator to the basement. Unlocking the door to the control room he entered, enjoying the hum of the machines. He had been running system checks for about two hours when the security alarm sounded. Jon hurried to the monitor in time to watch two men climb through the now broken lobby windows. To his horror he noticed Reggie sneak around a corner in the lobby. Why was he on the ground floor? Jon wondered, rushing for the elevator, changing his mind when he realized he had returned it to the 25th floor. He ran for the stairs bounding up them two at a time. As he burst through the door into the lobby, he heard Reggie screaming to be let go. Rounding the corner, he watched the kidnappers attempting to shove Reggie through the broken windows. Jon's feet felt like lead weights, like he was moving in slow motion. He didn't realize that in a matter of seconds he was jumping through those same broken windows the intruders had managed to push Reggie through. As he landed on the sidewalk he glanced in all directions and the street was vacant. Jon reined in his raging emotions managing to calmly call 911 informing them of what was happening. He quickly climbed back through the broken windows, forgetting he had the keys to the door, and rushed to go tell his father what was happening. To his surprise his father was walking slowly toward him.

"What's going on?" he snapped at Jon.

Jon replied, "Someone broke in and kidnapped Reggie."

"How? Where was he?" Amos yelled in panic.

"I saw him on the monitor when the alarm went off. He was in the lobby." Jon told his father, remaining calm even though he wanted to throw up. "Dad, wait here for the police. I'm going to turn off the alarms." And Jon left his father standing alone in the cold lobby as he rushed back to the control room.

Amos managed to make it to one of the seats near the information desk. Reggie had been kidnapped. How had this happened? He should never have allowed him to come today with the world in such turmoil. His ego had been so inflated with pride when Reggie had asked to come, he couldn't refuse him and now he was gone. Anguish washed over him causing a great pain to settle on his heart. He hadn't been able to save Christopher and now he had allowed this to happen to Reggie.

As soon as the alarms quieted, Amos heard the police sirens and when Jon reentered the lobby Amos was directing them to come through the windows.

Jon yelled, "Wait a minute! I'm here with the keys." And he rushed to open the front doors.

Two Seattle police officers walked inside and listened quietly to Jon as he explained what had happened. One stepped away and Jon heard him talking on his phone requesting a crime scene investigation team come help with the investigation.

After the police left, Jon suggested he lock up and they return home. His father readily agreed. It was another quiet trip home, as they headed across the Evergreen Point Floating Bridge, Jon, thinking how ironic that their world was being destroyed, while the waters of Lake Washington looked so placid. It should be raging as his emotions were raging. He was going to find out who had done this he promised himself.

Jon sat at his computer going through a secret list he had of several marines he had worked with in Iraq whom he knew would help him. He decided he would start with Captain Clay Patterson. They had been together for most of his tour of duty in Iraq and Jon trusted him. He dialed his number.

Clay answered on the first ring, "Hey, Jon!" he said way too cheerfully.

Jon replied, "Hi, Clay."

Clay hearing the despair in Jon's voice asked seriously, "What's wrong?"

"I need you, Clay, if you are available. My brother Reggie has been kidnapped."

"Oh, man! I'm sorry. How can I help?"

"I need help trying to track down who did this?"

"Sure. I'm not busy at the moment. I'll text you when I'll arrive at SEA TAC."

"Thanks."

"See ya in a few." And Clay hung up.

Jon sighed as he leaned forward placing his head in his hands and fought the despair that threatened to overpower him. He had to find Reggie! Two hours later Clay texted him he was arriving at SEA TAC tomorrow at noon. Jon headed downstairs to go find his family. He found his parents in the solarium talking quietly.

He entered, saying, "I just wanted to let you both know I have a friend from the Marines coming in tomorrow to help me try to find Reggie. I give you my word, I will find him!"

Amos cautioned, "Be careful, Jon."

"I will. I am going back into Seattle tonight so I can pick up my friend tomorrow. Do you need anything before I leave?"

Jon was worried about them. His mother just sat there sobbing quietly and his father had the look of a man who had lost all hope. Amos just shook his head "No" and neither parent spoke to him as he turned to leave.

The drive into Seattle was uneventful and he quickly had the Ferrari safely parked in the parking garage. He was glad the power had been restored and in moments he was in his penthouse sitting in front of his computer gazing at Agamemnon's name. Agamemnon. Should he try to reach him? Or even involve him in this mess? Jon knew he had left the marines shortly after him, but his career path had been much different than Jon's. Jon sighed, deciding that for now he would be better off without Agamemnon in his life. He would rely on Clay's help for the time being, hoping the kidnapping would be resolved quickly and Reggie would return home.

CHAPTER 8

Jon awoke the next morning after a terrible night's sleep where dreams of Iraq and Reggie mingled into a hellish nightmare of death and destruction. He hurried to the bathroom and took two aspirin hoping it would ease his pounding head. Grabbing a cup of coffee, he made his way to the windows in the living room, opening the blinds and gazed at what remained of the Ferris wheel. No fires smoldered this morning and he noticed more people seemed to be moving in the streets below. Maybe things would return to normal, he hoped.

Jon was surprised to discover that the airport seemed to be operating normally. He quickly realized no planes had actually crashed at the airport so when the government decided it was once again safe to fly, it had quickly been up and running. With all the destruction, Jon was amazed that the worlds computer and satellite systems did not seem to be affected. Everything seemed to be running smoothly.

After about an hour delay Clay finally came through the gates smiling at Jon. He was of average height, still fit and trim, his brown hair cut in the typical Marine style. Dark brown eyes twinkling with happiness, he declared, "At your service!"

Jon was always amazed at Clay's easy-going attitude. Sometimes it was hard to reconcile the man with the marine Jon knew him to be. Clay took all he did very seriously, and Jon thought he was a tad obsessive, like a hound with his nose stuck to the ground hunting a scent, he would not give up until the job was done right. Clay was not afraid to get his hands dirty, even kill when necessary. He was exactly who Jon needed at this moment.

They didn't talk until they were in Jon's car. Clay was astonished when Jon led him to the red Ferrari, but made no comment, realizing maybe he didn't know Jon as well as he thought he had. They had never discussed their private lives when in the service.

As the car slowed Clay glanced around at the neighborhood of modern skyscrapers, again surprised by where Jon seemed to live. Jon swung the car into a private parking space in the parking garage and led Clay toward a private elevator. When they entered the elevator, Clay noticed it went to one floor only, the 40th floor. He silently glanced at Jon who smiled at him. Quickly they were at the 40th floor and the doors opened on Jon's penthouse. Clay followed him into a home the likes of which he had only seen in movies or magazines. He was stunned and again glanced at Jon who was walking toward the kitchen. For the first time since he had met Jon in Iraq, he was wondering who he was.

"Want a drink?" Jon asked.

"Yeah, sure."

"I've got water, Coke or beer."

"Water is fine," Clay replied. Wanting to keep a clear head, he would not drink a beer now. Jon handed a cold bottle of water to Clay, who asked, "What's all this, Jon?" He swept his arm wide to indicate the penthouse.

"My home."

"Why was your brother kidnapped?" Clay asked, worried about the answer. Who was Jon and why did he drive a Ferrari and live in a place like this?

Jon, sensing Clay's concern said, "Clay, do you know anything about Prism Technologies?"

"Yeah, sure. Doesn't everyone?"

Jon chuckled. "Yes, I guess they do. Do you know who owns the company?"

"Yes again. It's that Sadler guy." Clay looked at him with astonishment. "Sadler. Your name is Sadler. No way!" He shook his head. "Really?!"

"Yes, really, that Sadler guy is my father and that's why Reggie was kidnapped," Jon said with dismay.

"I'm sorry, man."

"That's why I called you. I know you can help me track down who has done this. Come on I want to show you something," Jon said leading Clay to his office. "I need an extra mind that can think of things I might miss. You'll find everything I have managed to discover in that notebook beside the computer. You have complete access to the computer." He turned to leave the office. "Come on, I'll show you your room." Clay followed him to a large bedroom.

Jon continued. "We'll leave in a couple hours to head on over to my parents, home. I would like for you to meet them. I told them you would be helping me."

"Ok. I'll be ready. If it's ok with you I think I'll go to your computer and glance over what you have discovered so far."

"Sounds great to me. I'm going to make a quick check on the office building. I won't be long. Make yourself at home."

"See ya later," Clay said as he walked back to the office.

Clay was impressed with the progress Jon had made so far. He also noticed Jon had looked up Agamemnon, hoping he wasn't seriously thinking of contacting him. Clay was concerned it was Agamemnon who might be behind the kidnapping.

Clay became so engrossed in his search, he failed to hear Jon enter the penthouse, jumping when Jon called out, "Anybody home?"

Pushing back from the desk he was standing up when Jon entered his office saying, "Wow, I didn't realize it was so late. Using your computer is amazing." He glanced at Jon. "I had no idea the internet could do so much."

Jon grinned. "Yea, some of the perks of knowing my dad."

Clay laughed. "The next time I have a date I'm coming over here to investigate her."

"You sure about that? Sometimes knowledge isn't all it's cracked up to be."

"Just kiddin. I think I'll stick to the old-fashioned way of doing things."

"So seriously, did you discover anything?"

Clay replied with disappointment, "Nothing, Jon. No one is saying anything about the kidnapping. I was wondering, is there any place we can go where we might hear rumors about criminal activity?"

"Clay, I don't know, but I have been in touch with some questionable people searching for supplies, maybe I can contact them."

Clay gazed at him uncomfortably. "Like Agamemnon?"

"No Clay, I haven't been in contact with Agamemnon." Jon sensing Clay's unease continued, "Clay, I need to tell you everything. Let's take a seat in the living room and I'll tell you the whole story."

"Ok." Clay replied cautiously, following Jon, sitting across from him, waiting.

Jon began, "Fifteen years ago my father bought a bunker in the mountains of Virginia insisting the world was descending into chaos. He has been working on it for the last five years getting it ready for the apocalypse he insists is coming, and I have been working secretly over the last few months getting our arsenal together. My father would not be pleased if he knew, but I figure we may need the supplies to defend ourselves and I have made contact with some men who are helping me with the supplies, and I hope they might be able to help us find Reggie. My family plans on going to the bunker when Reggie has been returned and I'll be accompanying them to the bunker when they decide to leave. My father doesn't like that plan either, but he'll get over it. If you feel comfortable, I would like for you to accompany us to the bunker. My little brother really was kidnapped and is being held for ransom and I could use your help."

Clay quietly assessed what he had been told, wondering if he should trust Jon. Even though his wariness of Jon was making him uncomfortable, he knew from experience Jon was an honest man, so Clay said, "I think I'll wait to make a final decision after I meet your family."

Jon breathed a sigh of relief. He knew Clay would regain his trust when he met the family.

An hour later Clay was once again stunned when large black wrought iron gates were swinging open on the biggest home he had ever seen. It was a mansion. It was one thing to be aware people lived like this, but completely overwhelming to be faced with the reality. He quietly exited the Ferrari waiting for Jon to join him, then followed him into the mansion. Walking through the oversized front doors they entered an enormous foyer dominated by a huge staircase. Jon led him through a formal dining room, past a kitchen that seemed as big as his whole house and into an informal family room where the family was waiting. Clay watched an old man struggle to get to his feet, while a beautiful middle-aged woman waited patiently by his side. Using a cane, the bent over old man made his way toward Clay who was thinking the way the man was moving must be causing great pain, but he did not voice his thoughts. The man extended his free hand toward Clay.

Jon said, "My parents, Amos and Betty Sadler, and this is my friend Clay Patterson whom I was telling you about."

Clay shook Amos' hand and glanced at Mrs. Sadler when she reached for his hand, intrigued by the gentle, comforting woman who gazed at him with such compassion.

She spoke softly. "Welcome, Clay, we are glad you could make it."

Next, Jon directed his attention to his sisters and when Katie glanced at Clay with her soft grey eyes, he knew instantly he was going to the bunker with this family. Butterflies erupted in his stomach when she said, "We are glad to meet you, Clay."

He was excited and mortified at the same time, this had never happened to him in his entire life. How could a person fall in love at first sight? But that is exactly what was happening to him. He was crazy, he told himself. He desperately hoped no one in the room could see what was happening. Not only was the group unaware of Clay's feelings but Katie was completely oblivious.

Betty Sadler said, "Come, have a seat and we can visit until dinner is ready."

They all sat back down and asked polite questions of him. Clay honestly answered all questions asked of him, even when he told them of his parents dying when he was a teenager, and he went to live at a boys' home. They asked how he knew Jon and he told them they had met in Iraq, but did not elaborate, that was information better left in the past. No need to dredge up the nightmare that had been the war in Iraq. Jon knew and that was enough. He was pleasantly surprised when Jon's family asked no further questions about Iraq.

Completely by accident Katie was seated next to Clay at the dinner table and Betty quickly realized Clay was interested in her Katie which caused concern, because they did not know this man. She would make sure they didn't sit near each other again. The meal finished, the family once again returned to the family room to talk, Jon telling them they needed to head back to Seattle and work on finding Reggie. Good-byes were said and they were quickly back at Jon's penthouse, Clay telling him he would go with him to the bunker when it was decided they should leave.

CHAPTER 9

"So." Clay said, "How about we go someplace where we might learn where your brother might be."

"Sure." Jon replied trying to think of such a place, finally remembering a bar near the wharf. He wasn't sure it was still open after the plane crash, so he suggested they go for a walk to find out.

Strapping his Glock 19 under his jacket, he offered Clay his choice of the remaining handguns. He was not surprised when Clay chose the Browning Hi Power Classic. Both men loaded and secured their weapons then headed out into the now dark city of Seattle, glad to see there was no evidence of riots tonight, carefully making their way to the wharf.

The booming beat of the blaring music greeted them first, and they realized the bar was open. Jon had only driven by the place a few times but could not remember it being so appallingly tawdry. Jon and Clay paused in shocked disbelief when they rounded the corner of the building to see people in various stages of undress moving in an obscene undulating group to the beat of the music, apparently oblivious to the spectacle they were making of themselves.

Jon glanced at Clay. "Well, it's still open. Do you want to go inside?"

"Sure, why not?"

Taking a deep breath, they headed toward the entrance pushing through the seething mass of humanity. Entering the bar, they stopped to take in the surroundings. The bar was dark, the only light coming from several lights flashing in time to the pounding music.

Clay leaned close to Jon yelling. "I don't think we can learn anything here."

Jon agreed with a nod of his head, and they turned to push their way back through the crowd. A woman grabbed Clay around the neck almost knocking him off his feet. Shoving her away, he caused several of the crowd to lose their balance and tumble to the ground. Menacingly, the beast that had been lurking inside the crowd roared to life and lunged toward Jon and Clay intent on retribution.

"Run!" Clay yelled as Jon joined him in their attempt to escape the now violent crowd. Someone tripped Clay who hit the ground hard with a loud grunt.

Jon skidded to a halt whipping out his pistol flashing it at the crowd. "STOP! Or I'll shoot!"

The riotous crowd paused, as someone laughed. "Yeah, so what?"

Clay jumped back to his feet, as he too pointed his pistol at the crowd. "Just let us go and no one gets hurt!"

The second gun aimed at the crowd seemed to make them reconsider their attack on the two men and they returned to their dancing in front of the bar.

Jon and Clay walked slowly along the wharf searching for anyplace that might be open and finally, admitting defeat, they returned to Jon's penthouse.

"I think I'll go search the internet for restaurants in the area and see if any are opening after the rioting," Clay said when they entered Jon's home. He just couldn't sit around doing nothing.

"Sounds like a great idea. We should've thought of that before we went out tonight." Jon admitted wearily, lashing out in frustration, "I just want to find Reggie now!"

"I know Jon, I'll try my hardest to discover who has kidnapped him."

"Thanks. I appreciate the help. I think I'm going to bed. I'm exhausted."

"Will I bother you if I stay up?"

"No. Stay up as long as you want." Jon answered, walking to his room.

Clay went into the office and started to search restaurants first, then again searched the men he thought might be involved starting with Agamemnon. He was disappointed when Agamemnon came up clean again. Clay reluctantly admitted to himself he was not involved. He reviewed the police reports Jon had on file which still left him in the dark, they had not made any progress with the case. It was almost like Reggie didn't exist. This was going to be difficult.

Over the next few days, they went to several bars and restaurants without any success. They still could not find out where Reggie was being held. Every day they went over to Jon's parent's house hoping for a phone call from the kidnappers and every evening they ventured out into the city.

CHAPTER 10

A week after the kidnapping the kidnappers finally called. Amos answered the phone and listened, then said, "I'll not talk with you unless you let me speak to my son."

Jon signaled for his father to turn on the speakerphone, fear settling on Jon and his parents when quiet was all that greeted them. Every few seconds Amos yelled, "Hello? Let me talk to my son!"

Eventually, someone yelled back, "Shut up, old man, or we'll make you listen while we torture your son!"

Amos suddenly felt very old and useless, even after the accident he hadn't felt old, crippled, but not old. He reluctantly did as he was told, when he really wanted to reach through the phone and strangle everyone involved with this nightmare.

Abruptly, a breathless Reggie spoke, "Dad?"

"Reggie!" Amos said. "Are you ok, son?"

Betty took a sharp breath when Reggie's voice, sounding tired and weak, came through the phone. "I'm ok, Dad. Tell Mom I love her, and Dad...don't blame God."

One of the kidnappers yelled as he ripped the phone from Reggie. "Now, pay up old man. Two million dollars. We'll be in touch." And the phone went dead.

Jon held his mother as she sobbed uncontrollably, Amos paced around the room mumbling to himself. Chloe and Katie wandered in and stopped in the doorway, Chloe asking, "What's wrong?"

"The kidnappers just let Reggie speak to Dad, he put it on speaker phone and Mom could hear his voice. They are demanding two million dollars."

Chloe agonized, first Jim and the twins, now this with Reggie. When would the nightmare end? She watched silently as her father stormed from the room realizing he too was having difficulty coping. They all were.

Another week went by without any success finding Reggie, when the phone ringing startled everyone. Amos answered, "Yes, this is Amos Sadler."

Everyone watched silently as Amos listened. Dread settled on Jon when his father roared into the phone, "Who do you think you are playing with? I'll not give you anything! Let my son go and I won't prosecute you!"

Amos threw the phone across the room. "They hung up on me!"

By now Betty was sobbing quietly. Chloe and Katie wrapped their arms around their mother's shoulders and comforted her.

Jon told his father, "Dad, just give them the money."

Amos Sadler lashed out with anger so intense Jon backed away from him for the first time in his life. "Whose side are you on?"

Jon knowing all about feeling helpless and angry, said quietly, "Dad, please, you are upsetting Mom."

He knew his father would not believe him if he told him he understood so he hoped reminding him that his wife was still in the room would help calm him.

Amos' children watched their father glance at their mother with a despair so overwhelming it frightened them. Then he plopped down on the couch beside her and glancing toward his feet leaned his head in his hands. Betty gently put her arm around Amos' shoulders as he turned toward her and cried silently. Fear and anguish settled on Jon and his sisters at the sight of their father's tears. Turning they left them alone with each other.

Once they were in the kitchen Katie sat at the table and cried as Chloe pleaded desperately, "Jon isn't there something you can do?"

Jon's inability to discover any information about Reggie left him with feelings of frustration that were at dangerous levels. "I've been trying, Chloe!"

Suddenly he heard a vehicle squealing wheels as it sped away. "Stay here Chloe, Katie! I'm going to investigate, and I don't want you getting hurt," he commanded, running outside.

Jon and Clay ran toward the locked main gate, stopping long enough to enter the security code, running past the gate when opened and coming to a halt, Jon dropped to his knees with a gut wrenching, soul crushing "NO!!!" Clay noticed instantly what was going on and rushed back to the house to keep the rest of the family from going down to the driveway. When he went to get a security guard, he didn't realize one was already on his way and that Chloe had run out of the house to follow the guard. He yelled at Chloe to come back but she ignored him, so he continued into the house to keep the rest of Jon's family away from the nightmare in the driveway.

In a crumpled heap, beaten and bleeding, lay the shattered body of Jon's little brother. They had beaten his face severely but made sure not to completely destroy it, leaving enough intact to prove who he was, wanting to inflict as much pain as possible on Amos Sadler. His arms and legs lay twisted and contorted into unnatural angles while the blood seeped from the wounds on his torso. Jon, in a panic, searched for a pulse or breath of life without success. He knew from his time in Iraq there was no hope for Reggie. He grabbed Reggie's lifeless body and holding him to his chest he rocked and cried loudly over and over, "No, No, No!"

Chloe and one of the security guards found him rocking Reggie. Chloe screamed an ear-splitting scream as she too knelt beside Reggie pleading, "Do something, Jon! Do something!"

Jon ignored her, unable to react through his pain. The security guard called the police and stood at attention monitoring their surroundings and when another security guard appeared, he directed him to go back up to the house to deter Mr. and Mrs. Sadler from seeing Reggie. The police arrived, sirens blaring, and one officer squatted in front of Jon who still rocked Reggie, while his partner talked briefly with the security guard and then made his way to the mansion to run interference with the Sadler's.

Next the ambulance was pulling up as the neighbors were gathering around the scene. One EMT gently touched Jon on the shoulder, the police officer saying, "Mr. Sadler, please let the EMT's help."

Jon tried to focus on the men before him, but his eyes blurred from crying, made that impossible. He heard someone sobbing and glanced around to find another police officer holding Chloe. Suddenly, he thought of his parents. He gently released Reggie and stood up demanding, "Where are my parents?"

"They are with Officer Taylor up at the house. We are not allowing them to come down here," the officer with him said.

"Thank you," Jon replied stepping away from his brother as the EMT's rushed forward and Officer Wilson handed him a handkerchief saying, "I think you need this."

Jon wiped his face and for the first time noticing the crowd watching, lashed out aggressively. "What are you all looking at!" he yelled. "Leave now!"

He lunged toward the crowd as Officer Wilson stepped in front of him. "Mr. Sadler, it's not their fault. Stay here and I'll talk to them." He turned and dispersed the crowd.

Within minutes they had Reggie's body covered with a sheet on the stretcher and were loading him into the ambulance as the police officers were placing the yellow crime scene tape all around the front of the mansion.

Jon walked up to Chloe taking her hand, whispered, "Come on, let's go back up to the house."

Chloe glanced at him with wide eyed horror. "Jon, you can't let Mom and Dad see you like that."

He paused, looking down at himself and started to shake uncontrollably. He was covered from his neck to his knees in Reggie's blood. Leaving Chloe standing alone in the middle of the driveway he ran toward the back of the mansion and entering the kitchen grabbed a trash bag and ran upstairs to his room. Removing the clothes, he stuffed everything he had on into the trash bag, tying it shut and stepped into the shower. He scrubbed and scrubbed his body and washed his hair several times and then just stood under the streaming water letting it pound his body hoping it would wash away the nightmare. Nothing in the Marines had prepared him for this. Gradually he became aware someone was knocking on his bedroom door yelling for him. He turned off the shower and drying quickly threw on the first things he grabbed and answered the door.

Officer Wilson stood beside his father, "Mr. Sadler I'm sorry, I do understand how horrible this is, but I need to talk with you while your memories are fresh."

Jon followed the officer and his father to Amos' private office.

Detective Farland, who had followed them into the room, asked, "Mr. Sadler do you have any enemies?"

Both Jon and his father gazed at the detective in alarmed silence, Jon asking, "Why would you ask a question like that?"

"Because this is a crime of passionate hate. Someone who hates your family tortured Reggie to death. This is not a typical crime."

Jon glanced at his father who was staring at the detective in horrified silence, then Jon replied with appalling disbelief. "We don't know of anyone who hates us. Especially, hates us enough to murder Reggie."

"Well, if either of you can think of anyone who might have threatened you or who you have made very angry, please let me know." The police officer and detective offered their condolences as they turned to leave.

Amos showed the men the way out, leaving Jon sitting very still gazing out the window, as a burning anger, dark and deep, settled on his soul. He could not think of anyone who hated his family enough to do what they had done to Reggie, and he promised himself he would kill everyone involved with Reggie's murder. He began forming preliminary plans. He knew the police would not be able to catch those who had done this quickly enough for his satisfaction, but he would use them to help him gain information, and he just might go to Agamemnon for help.

His thoughts were interrupted when his father re-entered the room. Walking slowly toward Jon, he sat down near him. His only surviving son, thought Amos, and he knew that he was not going to stop Jon from seeking vengeance. He knew his son well enough to know that the anger simmering in his soul might destroy him, but he also knew he could not stop him, so he whispered, "Be careful Jon."

Jon turned eyes as cold as blue ice toward his father. "I will, Dad. But first I'll go with you to the bunker and make sure you're all settled in and everything is working correctly."

"We'll manage fine," Amos said.

"I'm still going with you."

Amos felt his ire rising and declared, "I said we'll be fine. You just do what you need to do."

Amos was ready to explode when Jon smiled at him smugly. "I'm going, Dad!" he replied with a calm that enraged his father.

"I said No!"

Jon shrugged his shoulders and Amos roared, "You will do as I say!" and stood up to walk from the room.

Jon let him go, knowing his mother would agree with him and tell him when his father planned on leaving and he would be there. Standing up, he went in search of his mother to tell her what was going on and of his plans to go back into Seattle tonight.

CHAPTER 11

Clay chose to stay with Katie, so Jon drove himself into Seattle and stopped by the Seattle Police headquarters, parking his Ferrari between two police cars hoping it would be safe there. Entering the building his nose was assaulted with the odors of stale coffee, various human body odors, and floor wax.

Making his way to the front desk he said, "I'm Jon Sadler. I would like to talk to the person in charge of my brother Reggie Sadler's investigation, please."

The officer pointed to some chairs near the wall across from the desk and told Jon to have a seat. Jon picked up an old magazine, pretending to read, but he was on high alert listening to everything around him. A few cops were laughing and cursing about something, a woman was crying and yelling she hadn't done anything wrong, while another cop was manhandling a drunken man through a door, to a holding cell Jon assumed. Suddenly, another door swung open and a large rotund police officer called his name. Jon stood and walked toward the man, extending his hand for a handshake. Jon fought the urge to jerk his hand back from the large damp hand which limply made a pretense at shaking his hand. Jon was repulsed by the police Captain. Is this what the Seattle police had become? He knew they must be overwhelmed with the aftermath of the disappearance of so many people and the rioting, but there seemed to be a feeling of uncaring indifference and it showed in the dirt and crumpled disarray of the police personnel and the station. How had things changed so quickly?

After stating his concerns, Jon quickly realized he would get no help from the police and finally stood up saying, "Thank you, Captain. I'll appreciate any information you can give me about the investigation."

Jon couldn't bring himself to offer his hand for another handshake and was relieved the Captain didn't seemed inclined to shake his hand either. The Captain dismissed him nonchalantly saying, "We'll do what we can to help you."

Jon walked back outside and paused to glance around. The change was almost palatable, the feeling of dread which had washed over him on the day of the earthquake was pressing in on him. He felt surrounded by evil. He decided he needed to go to his penthouse and pack some supplies, so he would be ready when the time came for the trip he was making with his family to the bunker.

He was home quickly and stood gazing out the windows in the living room lost in his anguished thoughts. He turned from the windows as the sky darkened with sunset, pushing the switch on the remote control which caused the shades to lower, blocking out the world. If only it were so easy, he thought to himself, to shut out the world.

He grew restless as the night wore on, the anger gnawing at his soul, until he needed to find release, deciding he would revisit some of the places Clay and he had been to, he strapped the holster on his hip, loaded his pistol, placing it in the holster and strapped his knife's sheath around his shoulder, sliding the blade into position under his left armpit. He gazed at his reflection in the mirror and was pleased with the beard he was letting grow which completely covered his lower face. He would be glad when his hair finally grew longer too. He was hoping he would not be easily recognizable while he was searching for those who had murdered Reggie.

He knew it was dangerous to venture out without Clay, but at the moment he didn't care, he desperately needed to be doing something that would help him exact his vengeance. Dressed in worn out jeans and a flannel shirt, he was quickly exiting the building. He paused to look around, and noticed a shimmering orange glow to the north; he realized the rioters had started again, setting something on fire. He made a snap decision to wander down toward Pioneer Square. He and Clay had agreed they would visit the underground city when they returned from the bunker, but he decided tonight was the night to see what he could discover about what might be going on in the underground city. He made his way toward the underground door and was surprised to find it unlocked and guarded by a fat man who appeared more than a little drunk.

The man sneered at Jon. "What's your pleasure? It's gonna cost you 50 to enter."

Jon said nothing, just pulled a 50-dollar bill from his pocket and handed it to the man who then decided since Jon had been so easy he would demand more.

"I changed my mind. It's 50 more." He coughed sending a cloud of his putrid breath Jon's way.

Jon fought gagging and whipped his knife out. "You sure about that? Maybe I'll take my 50 back and all the rest of the money you have."

The large man backed far out of Jon's reach mumbling, "I didn't mean no harm. Just kiddin."

Jon stepped through the door, making his way to the street below. His senses were assaulted by the rank smell of marijuana, unwashed bodies, and human excrement. The smell was so intense it burned Jon's nostrils, amazing him how fast the dregs of society had moved into the underground city filling it full of trash and filth. He walked carefully in the middle of the centuries old road passing people passed out or possibly dead, those shooting up or smoking their poison, and couples satisfying their needs on the sidewalks. Several people, both men and women propositioned him, but he abruptly refused, cursing at them, knowing if he wanted to stay alive, he had to appear as hard and debauched as they were. He wandered into what appeared to be a makeshift drug house and sat down at the bar. Quickly an anorexic thin woman whose face was marred with the pock marks of her life of sin and drug addiction, sat beside him. The smell of her profession hung about her in a cloud of stench that turned Jon's stomach and before he could move away, her hand grabbed his crouch.

"Not today!" Jon said harshly pushing her hand away.

She cursed at him and stumbled to the next man at the bar. Jon acquired the drink he had ordered and noticing an empty table in a corner, went to sit down and sip his drink. He had no intentions of getting even slightly drunk in this place. He would watch and listen tonight hoping he might hear something useful. After a couple hours without any success, knowing no more than when he entered the underground city, the smell making him sick as his fatigue started to settle on him, he decided he needed to leave while he was still alert and made his way back outside where he stopped when he had walked a few feet from the entrance, and breathed deeply of the fresh night air. He quickly realized as he walked home that the stench of the underground city was sticking to him like glue. When his private elevator stopped at his penthouse, he stripped naked before leaving the elevator and making his way to the kitchen grabbed a trash bag and returned to the elevator, bagging everything he had been wearing for disposal in the trash. He left the bag in the elevator and shutting the door went to take a much needed shower. After the shower he curled up in bed and slept until 3 p.m.

He came awake promptly, temporarily disoriented having no idea what time it was or even what day it was. Running his hand through his hair he stood up, making his way to the living room windows and gazed out at the placid waters of Elliot Bay. It still made him angry that nature seemed to move along so calmly while his emotions raged. As he became more alert, he realized he was due to meet his family at the funeral home to make final arrangements for his brother. Dressing quickly, he was at his parents' home just in time to ride with them. The agony of what they were all going through burned in Jon's gut. He couldn't image what his parents were suffering.

The next day dawned sunny and warm. It was as if nature was laughing at their heartache by making such a glorious day to bury Reggie. Jon's anger raged as he dressed, raged at the evil injustice that had taken one such as Reggie, a gentle kind soul. Why hadn't the evil ones who had tortured him to death been taken?

Then Jon was stunned to watch his mother. She exited the limo with a sad smile, Jon wondering how she could be smiling, then she spoke softly. "Isn't it beautiful. It's as if Reggie is telling us he loves us and is with us, giving us such a beautiful day."

He realized that she needed to find comfort somehow in the midst of such heartache and he wrapped his arm around her shoulders holding her close, as he led her to the graveside. Hundreds of people crowded around the family, Chloe sobbing loudly and Katie watching in distressed silence as fat tears rolled down her cheeks. Amos Sadler made his way slowly to a seat near the casket, the weight of his sorrow making him appear even more bent over and crippled. Jon helped his mother to the seat beside his father and sat down next to Katie and never heard a word the unknown preacher said. Where did this man come from anyway? This man who had never met Reggie? Who had told him to be here? He would discover later that Chloe had invited him to speak because he had been the preacher her husband Jim had known. Right now, Jon was so enraged and bitter he was desperately trying to keep his mouth shut and not yell at everyone to just leave them alone. His love for his surviving family motivated him to sit quietly through this hell on earth.

The funeral, over they drove back home with Jon telling his family he was going into Seattle as he turned and quickly walked to his Ferrari and was gone.

CHAPTER 12

The next afternoon when Jon was visiting his family the phone rang and he answered it, to hear a strange unknown voice ask, "Is this Jon Sadler?"

"Who's asking?" Jon demanded evasively.

A wicked chuckle was followed by. "Oh, just a friend who is wondering how you liked what happened to your little brother?" Jon fighting feelings of disgust and intense rage couldn't find the words to answer, so the unknown caller continued. "I'm not through with your family. I will be given another chance to kill again. Maybe your mother or one of your sisters."

Jon hammered the phone onto the cradle disconnecting the call. When the phone rang again, he quickly picked it up and slammed it back down, realizing Detective Farland had been right. Someone hated his family. But why?

His father yelled, "Who was on the phone?"

"Wrong number, Dad." Jon lied, because he had no intention of telling his family about the call.

A week later the family decided it was time to go to the bunker, and Clay had called asking Jon to come get him so he could pack for the trip. When they returned to the penthouse Jon did research on the computer while Clay packed and then watched TV.

The next morning Jon ignored his father when he bounded onto the waiting jet, followed by Clay.

"I told you not to come!" Amos roared at him.

Jon smiled at his furious father and sat down next to Chloe who had her face buried in a magazine completely ignoring the commotion between her brother and father, while Clay sat down next to a smiling Katie.

Jon smiled at his mother when Betty said softly, "I'm glad you made it, Jon and Clay."

Amos harrumphed under his breath and turned away from everyone to look out the window as the jet started to taxi down the runway. The flight was silent as everyone was still trying to understand what was happening in their lives and the world and were tired of talking about it.

When they landed in Roanoke, Jon told them he had business to attend to and he would be right back. Amos stood glaring at his son as he marched away from him wondering what he was up to; Jon returned few minutes later, riding in a golf cart. "Hop on board, everyone."

Once everyone was on board Amos demanded, "Where are we going?"

Jon pretended not to hear him, knowing if he told him what was going on his father would get off the golf cart. The automatic doors slid open to the outside, and the driver drove them toward a waiting helicopter.

Amos roared, "What's going on, Jon!?"

Jon finally glared at his father. "We can no longer drive to the bunker, and I thought the helicopter would be more comfortable than going in on horseback."

"Have you lost your mind, Jon? Why can't we drive to the bunker?"

"Because I had the construction crew destroy the road and place boulders and plant trees to disguise it."

"Who authorized this?" Amos shouted.

Jon replied curtly. "I did!"

Before Jon could say more, everyone in the golf cart was stunned when Betty placed her hand on Amos' arm saying gently. "You have said enough, Amos. Jon is doing what he knows is best."

After Jon made sure everyone was seated and secure in the helicopter he climbed into the cockpit, placed the headset over his ears and waited for clearance to take off. Quickly permission was given, and Jon smoothly lifted the chopper into the air.

Amos remained quiet during the ride to the bunker, but everyone could sense his stewing anger. After Jon landed in a small clearing near the bunker, he made a phone call. Amos stepped from the helicopter unable to remain quiet any longer. "So, what do we do now? Sit here and watch the sunset?" he turned hard grey eyes toward Jon. "Or maybe we walk to the bunker?"

Before Jon could blow up, everyone turned toward the sound of clomping hooves to see a wagon being pulled by two horses. Jon couldn't take his father's hateful remarks any longer and stomped away toward the wagon, his father's sarcastic words following him. "So, now we are in the Wild West?"

When he drew close to the wagon he said, "Hi Fred" smiling up at the construction foreman. "Thanks for helping out again."

Then he whispered, "The old man is furious about the way things are going. Just try to ignore him. I'm going to walk to the bunker." And he marched away heading for the bunker.

Fred grinned widely saying, "Yes sir, Mr. Sadler."

Ignoring his father's angry yelling, Jon disappeared into the thick forest, thinking about his family's safety. He had made up his mind he was going to ask Clay if he could stay with his family at the bunker to help protect them while he was gone. One disabled man, and three women did not need to be left alone without adequate protection.

He waited at the back entrance to help unharness the horses and talk to Fred. He had important things to discuss with him. When the wagon arrived, Clay jumped to the ground and helped Amos down as Jon helped his mother into the bunker.

Jon said, "I'm going to help Fred with the horses. I'll be right in."

The rest of the group entered the bunker and Jon talked with Fred as they unharnessed the horses. "Fred, I have an important question to ask."

"Yes sir, Mr. Sadler."

"First, let's drop the Mr. Sadler. Jon is just fine."

Ok, Mr. um...I mean Jon."

"I need to know if you and your family are prepared to survive. I've been doing some reading and I think what is happening was written about in the Bible and things are only going to get worse. I want to make sure your family is safe. Do you have some place like this to escape to if needed?"

Fred grinned. "Yes, I do. I figured a couple years ago, that if one of the richest men in the world was making preparations like this, I needed to also. So, I purchased a prefab underground bunker myself and have everything ready if we need to bug out."

Jon was relieved. "Great, Fred! Now I feel better knowing you are prepared, but if you ever need me for anything you know you can always come to me for help."

"Thanks, Jon." He walked back outside.

Jon followed and watched him mount his own horse, saying, "I see you have a horse too."

"He's not mine. He belongs to my daughter. She barrel races, I figured it would be easier to ride in on horseback, so I borrowed him. Call me any time you need help getting in here. Take care, Jon," he replied turning the horse toward home.

"Thanks, Fred. You take care too," Jon called as he turned to enter the bunker.

As he walked into the living area Jon was pleased to see his mother investigating the kitchen and Clay and Katie moving furniture. Chloe must be checking out the bedrooms. His father was sitting in a Lazy Boy glaring at everyone.

When the object of Amos' dissatisfaction entered the bunker, he growled at him. "I still want to know what's all of this foolishness? Why destroy the road and make us have to use a helicopter, Jon?"

Jon took a slow deep breath, asking, "Do you want to be found, Dad?"

Amos made no reply, continuing to glare at Jon. Jon continued. "Why go through all of the expense to hide the bunker and leave the road intact so anybody could easily wander in and find us? The world has changed suddenly, I think the apocalypse you prepared for is upon us, Dad."

"I think maybe you are right, Jon," Amos mumbled in deep disappointment. He had to admit to himself he was no longer in control. He had never really been in control. He had domineered, dominated, coerced, and browbeat people and circumstances to fulfill his wishes but he had never really been in control. It was a sobering realization.

Jon helped Clay and Katie arrange the furniture as their mother wished and then asked Clay if he wanted to take a ride with him to check the property. Clay happily agreed, so the two men set out on horseback. Jon had ulterior motives for wanting to be alone with Clay.

When they were far enough away from the bunker Jon said, "Clay, I need to talk with you."

"Sure, what's up?"

"I'm heading back to Seattle to get started again on my investigation and I was wondering if you would be able to stay here and help take care of my family, until I return?"

"Jon I'll be happy to help out, but I need to return home and tie up some loose ends. I also have a few more leads I need to check out for your investigation."

Jon was disappointed but admitted to himself he had sprung this on Clay at the last minute and replied, "Great. We'll leave after we get the horses settled and decide when you'll return after we have taken care of business."

Both men returned to the bunker and told the family their plans. Jon noticed the way Katie was watching Clay and was surprised. He would not have thought Clay would have been a man she would be interested in. Fascinating he thought.

Within the hour they had re-boarded the helicopter and were taking the private jet back to Seattle. A few hours later they landed at SEA-TAC, Clay telling Jon he would be back in a few days, while Jon headed to the penthouse.

CHAPTER 13

Three days later Clay was pounding on the door to Jon's penthouse. When Jon opened the door, he was relieved to see Clay had returned so quickly. "Glad to see you," Jon said moving aside so Clay could enter.

"So, how soon will I be returning to the bunker?"

"I'll have the jet ready for you tomorrow morning. I need some help before you leave."

"Ok. Let's get started," Clay replied heading to the bedroom to leave his suitcases.

When he reentered the living room it was to find Jon silently gazing out of the large windows. Clay paused feeling a twinge of worry for his friend.

Jon swung around to face Clay with a look of such intense pain Clay felt uncomfortable witnessing his friend's distress and helpless about what to say, but Jon said first, "Like I said, I hope you can help me, Clay."

"I'll give it my best shot."

"Do you remember Agamemnon?"

Clay was overcome with foreboding, unhappy about Jon wanting to contact Agamemnon. He did not think Jon was aware of exactly who the man was and just how dangerous he could be.

He said with trepidation, "Yeah, I remember him. Why do you ask?"

"I was wondering if by chance you know how I can contact him."

Jon saw the almost imperceptible flinch as Clay attempted to pretend ignorance, and he glared at him with eyes cold as blue ice when Clay said evasively, "Sorry Jon, but I have no idea how to contact him."

Unaware, until this moment, he could be as ruthless as his father, Jon's hard eyes glinted at Clay with intense anger. "Really?" he said between clenched teeth.

Clay quickly realized two things. First, he didn't want to lose his friendship with Jon because of Agamemnon and second, he knew Jon was determined to go to Agamemnon no matter who helped him get there and this could cost him his life, so Clay decided he needed to help him. The proper information could save Jon's life.

Clay rushed ahead not giving Jon a chance to interrupt him. "Ok. I lied. I do know where Agamemnon is and how you can contact him. I lied because he is a very dangerous man, Jon, and will kill you as soon as talk to you."

Jon was struggling with his blinding rage. His commonsense self, told him Clay lied because he cared, but the self that craved to kill those involved with Reggie's murder threatened to erupt in violence. He silently went into his bedroom and locked the door. Clay watched him leave realizing Jon needed to be alone to calm down. He decided it would anger Jon even more if he did research on the computer, so he plopped down on the couch and started to watch a movie.

An hour later Jon walked into the living room and stopped when he saw Clay. Clay glanced up at Jon relieved to see the raging anger burning in his eyes gone. Jon sat down in one of the chairs near the couch and Clay wisely waited for Jon to speak.

"I know Agamemnon is dangerous. I know what he is capable of. You know we have not had any success finding Reggie's murderers, I think Agamemnon is the only one left who can help me. I'm desperate, Clay."

Clay knew a desperate man could be a sloppy man, and knowing he could not change Jon's mind, he offered him his knowledge. "He has a warehouse on the waterfront of Oakland which he uses to run his illegal drug cartel. I'll show you on a satellite map exactly where it is located and will give you the password to gain entrance. Make sure you have your weapons with you and do not give them up to anyone. Agamemnon will see you."

Jon was stunned. "How do you know this, Clay?"

Clay replied, "Let's just say, I also needed Agamemnon at one time." He refused to elaborate, and Jon didn't pressure him.

They spent the next hour going over the information Jon needed to know and when Clay was satisfied he had told Jon everything, he went to his bedroom. He needed time himself to calm his nerves after the afternoon he had spent with Jon.

The next morning Jon drove Clay to the airport, made sure he boarded the jet without difficulty, and gave him instructions on how to contact Fred. Now he must get down to the serious work of having his vengeance on Reggie's murderers. He decided he would make one more trip into the underground city before he contacted Agamemnon, hoping he could catch a break and wouldn't have to get involved with him.

RESCUE

CHAPTER 14

Jon took a deep breath of fresh air before he walked up to the same fat man guarding the entrance to the underground city. Without a word he handed him the 50-dollar admission fee and the man wisely let him pass un-accosted. Jon cautiously made his way to the same bar he had visited a week ago, plopping down on a barstool, pulling the baseball cap down low over his eyes hoping no one would recognize him. Glancing around he noticed a young woman, possibly a teenager, sitting on a barstool near the end of the bar who seemed to be trying to appear invisible. She glanced at Jon, and he smiled at her which caused her to quickly look away. Jon looked away and noticed out of the corner of his eye, the bartender walk over to the girl and angrily confront her. He watched her shiver and then glance at him again, smiling invitingly. Jon was repulsed and felt pity that such a young girl, because Jon felt sure she was just a girl, was being forced into a life of prostitution. He slowly stood up and walked over to her. As he drew closer to her, he was disgusted to realize her face was painted, causing her to look like a freak, with garish colors above her golden eyes, cheeks an unnatural pink and her lips bright red. The thin tank top she was wearing barely covered her upper body showing skin the color of buttery caramel, her black hair hung in tight ringlets to her shoulders. She glanced up at him with eyes full of fear and forced a smile.

She whispered without emotion. "It'll be $100 dollars for 20 minutes."

Jon was appalled that those words had been spoken by a child. He asked, "How old are you?"

She looked into his eyes with surprise. "Old enough," she stated flatly and stood up. "So, are you coming with me or not?"

Jon wanted to run away but forced himself to follow her through a door at the back of the bar which led to a long hall with several closed doors. The girl walked through an open door and closed it behind her after Jon entered and went to sit on the poor excuse for a bed. Stale, putrid air assaulted his nose and Jon, eyeing the disgusting bed, just knew it must be crawling with vermin.

"Money due up front," she demanded.

Jon took a 100-dollar bill from his pocket and handed it to her as he managed to work up enough nerve to sit down beside her.

She grew nervous, twisting her hands together while he sat quietly beside her staring at the wall across from them. "So, what do you want?" she finally asked.

Jon glanced at her, and the girl was again surprised by the blueness of his eyes. Eyes as cold as blue ice and he frightened her.

"I guess I just want to talk." he said, quickly concocting a cover story. "I lost my wife and little boy when all of those people disappeared."

He was thrilled to notice sympathy flit across her face before the hard, protective shell slipped back into place. "Ok, but you don't get your money back."

Jon knew they were being listened to and watched, so he rattled on about his pretend wife and little boy thinking about Reggie to make his story sound plausible.

He was relieved when she said, "Time is up." Jumping up from the bed, she walked to the door. Jon followed her back to the bar and left without saying a word.

The girl watched him walk away completely confused. She had never had a man just talk to her. It was a new and rather frightening experience. She wandered back over to her barstool and sat back down.

Jon forced himself to wait three days before he ventured back underground. He was hoping the girl would be there. He arrived at the bar to deep disappointment, finding the place almost empty and no girl. He grabbed a drink and went to sit in a corner to watch, hoping he was just early. After two hours he was planning on leaving when she walked up to her seat. Not caring if he came across as anxious, because he didn't want someone else to approach her first, he jumped up and went to sit on the barstool beside her.

He was surprised to see fear in her eyes when she noticed him walking toward her. He smiled and noticed her return smile did not reach her eyes. He sat down beside her and said, "Hi."

She whispered back, "Hi" and swallowed hard when the bartender headed their way and she said loud enough for him to hear, "What's your pleasure?"

Jon glanced up at the bartender and grinned like an idiot. Better for him to think he was an idiot than to think Jon was a threat.

"Everything, ok Trixie?" the man asked.

The girl shivered like the last time the bartender had spoken to her and replied, "Yes."

The bartender turned and walked away as Jon said, "So your name is Trixie?"

The girl looked at him with disgust. "You could say that."

"Well, if it isn't, then what is your name?"

"Mister, I ain't got time for small talk. Are you interested?"

Jon pulled a 100-dollar bill out of his pocket.

"Not here. Someone will kill you for the money. Put it back in your pocket and follow me."

They stood up and she led Jon to a different yet equally disgusting room down the same hall as the last time. They once again sat on the bed together as Jon slipped the money to her. When he tried to hand her the money, she wrapped her thin arms around his neck and snuggling her face into his neck she whispered in his ear. "You had better do something this time or you might get killed."

Jon was shocked and taken aback. He didn't want to do anything except rescue this slip of a girl. He wrapped his arms around her and held her close, whispering back, "Thanks."

He pushed her back on the bed and lay beside her and pretended he was interested in her as he softly ran his hand up her thin arm. Suddenly he jumped up almost knocking her into the floor as she squealed.

"I'm sorry!" he stuttered. "I'm not ready tonight. I just enjoyed talking last time. Maybe next time."

And he ran from the room. Leaving a totally confused Trixie gazing in stunned silence at the closed door. She squealed again when the door was slung open, and a large man walked into the room. His green eyes were sunk deep into his gaunt pale face and burned with an evil that terrified her. She watched him walk toward her wondering again why he moved in such an awkward fashion. He swung his legs out in front of him as if he had difficulty bending them at the knees. He stopped in front of her glaring at her with hate filled eyes.

"Are you losing your touch?" he hissed.

Fear made her feel like vomiting, but she managed to answer him. "I don't know what is wrong with him. He says his wife is dead."

"I know that you idiot. I heard him." his hand lashed out lightning fast, striking her hard across her left cheek. "If he comes again, you had better finish the job."

He turned and left the room as she quickly ran to the restroom and splashed water on her face to hide her tears. Within minutes she was back on her barstool.

CHAPTER 15

Tonight, was the night. It had taken Jon two days to get everything in order. He had finally found a car he had paid too much cash for. He kept the previous owner's license plates on the car and planned the escape route back to his penthouse along the alleyways and back streets. As he dressed for yet another trip into the underground city, he hoped Trixie would be brave enough to run away with him. He had been having nightmares about the girl. He could not begin to understand this driving need to rescue her. Maybe it was losing Reggie. He just didn't know.

He hoped this would be the last time he ever had to enter the nightmare that had become Seattle's famous underground city. He carefully parked the non-descript car in a nearby parking garage and walked toward the underground. Once again, he paid his entrance fee to the ever-present fat man and made his way to the bar, pleased to see Trixie sitting on her bar stool talking to a drunk customer. He walked up to Trixie and smiled but she looked at him with mortified anger. Stay alert, Jon told himself as he set down beside the man and quickly realized he was very drunk and could barely stand.

"Hi, Trixie," Jon said nonchalantly.

The man turned toward Jon, almost falling. "Go away. She is mine."

Jon pulled out the small switchblade knife, he had hidden, and gently poked it into the man's side, just enough for him to feel it but not cause any great harm, making him scream in pain and anger. The knife disappeared back into Jon's pocket as quickly as it had appeared just as the bartender made it to the scene.

The bartender hissed at the drunk stranger. "I told you to leave! I don't serve no drunks."

"Something is hurting," the drunk managed to mumble as he stumbled away from Trixie. "I didn't mean no harm." He managed to make it to the entrance and stumbled out the door.

Now the bartender turned eyes full of distain on Jon, saying, "I'm not sure you should stay here tonight. You have caused enough trouble."

Jon smiled. "I just wanted to see Trixie tonight. I didn't mean no harm, but if you want me to leave I will."

To Jon's shocked surprise her tiny hand rested on his left forearm, "It's ok, Bart. He can come with me."

"Ok, Trixie, if you feel safe with him."

Trixie wasn't sure how she felt around this man but getting a break from the horrors of her job and being paid to do so was hard to pass up. She stood up and the tall man with the piercing blue eyes followed her.

Jon was relieved when the situation deescalated quickly, and he was following Trixie down the hall once again. They entered a different room this time and he handed her the $100 and sat down beside her. Nervously, he hoped his plan would work. He wrapped his arms around her pushing her down on the bed and gently positioned himself over her.

He bent down as if to kiss her, sorry to see the revulsion and fear shinning in her eyes, as he whispered quickly in her ear, "I'm here to help. Just play along."

Trixie was almost sick with fear but remained still and quiet. Jon rested on one elbow as his free arm reached in between their bodies in the general direction of his pants zipper. She could feel him fumbling, pushing her skirt up and was overcome with despair. She had thought he was different. Then to her shocked surprise she felt his hand sliding up her shirt and felt something cold and hard shoved under her clothes onto her abdomen as he kissed her cheek.

"I promise I won't do anything to you or hurt you, but please play along. When we are done please meet me outside of the underground, I'll be waiting for you. Please come to me, Trixie." he whispered near her ear as he kissed her cheek again. To her surprise she wished he knew her real name.

She felt him move on top of her and realized what he was pretending to do, and she moaned when he suddenly stopped and rested on top of her. Nothing physically had happened between the two of them except for whatever he had stuffed in her clothes. This was the weirdest thing she had ever been through, and she was more than a little afraid.

He rolled off the bed pretending to adjust his pants saying, "You were great. I'll come see you again."

Then he turned and left the room, leaving her sitting on the bed in stunned silence. A voice came over the hidden intercom. "Get up and go back to work."

She stood up walking to the wall opposite the bed and opening a small door in the wall pushed the money through the opening, then made her way to the filthy bathroom, her curiosity overwhelming her. She had to see what he had stuffed in her clothes.

She entered, locking the door behind her and felt under her top as the tears started to flow down her cheeks. His was a kindness she had almost forgotten people could be capable of having. He had noticed she was barefoot and had slipped a pair of shoes into her clothes knowing she needed them to escape. All the girls were kept barefoot making it impossible to leave the brothel. She had had no intention of going to him until she found those shoes. She knew she could trust a person who was so concerned for her welfare, he had thought of her trying to run through the underground city streets on bare feet, with all the filth and broken glass, knowing it would slice her feet to shreds. Even pretending to rape her to keep her alive. She was overcome with emotion. She quickly wiped the tears away and left the bathroom heading away from the entrance to the bar knowing there was a back entrance into this hallway which exited to the alley behind the bar. To her surprise she made it out without incident or being discovered. She paused once she was in the alley to slip on the shoes. They were a tad small, but she didn't care. Freedom was just a couple blocks away. She had never been one to pray, but now she prayed God would help her to escape.

Jon quickly made his way back out of the entrance and was pleased to find the gate guard passed out. He slipped behind some trees near the entrance to wait. He realized she might be awhile so he would wait until daybreak. He was surprised when 20 minutes later she stumbled out of the door and stopped, her gaze searching the area around her. He stepped from behind the trees and grabbing her hand pulled her along with him trying to match his stride to hers as they ran the block toward the parking garage. Just before they entered the garage, she heard a sound that almost caused her to faint with terror. She heard them calling her, followed by dogs barking. She had been kidding herself, this man couldn't save her, she was going to die tonight. Jon ignored her silent tears and sudden inability to move when she heard her name and pulled her along toward the car. He must get her into the car. He jerked the passenger door open and pushed her inside as he climbed behind the steering wheel. Resisting the urge to speed, which would cause the wheels to squeal, and possibly give away their position, he calmly drove out of the garage and took the route he had previously set for himself. He parked the car in another parking garage two miles from the first. He told her they would walk the rest of the way. The going was slow as he refused to use a flashlight. He took her by the hand leading her toward his penthouse, staying in the alleyways and shadows of the tall buildings.

After they had walked a couple blocks, she whispered, "Where are we?"

"Near the Ferris Wheel."

"I mean, which city is this?"

He glanced at her in surprise. It had never dawned on him she had no idea where she was. "This is Seattle."

"Seattle, Washington?"

"Yes."

"Wow," she said breathlessly, "I'm from Idaho. I've never been to Seattle."

How many more surprises did she have for him, Jon wondered as he led her into the parking garage of his penthouse. They entered his private elevator quietly and were quickly at the 40th floor. Jon dreaded the thought of entering his penthouse dressed in the stinking clothes he had on, but he would not embarrass her by suggesting she strip in the elevator.

They stepped into his penthouse and Trixie gasped. "What is this place. Where are we?"

Jon looked around at the familiar surroundings of his penthouse and then glanced back at her, surprised to see her gazing around in wide eyed wonder.

He said, "Welcome to my home."

"This is yours?" she asked in disbelief.

Jon chuckled. "Yes, it is, and you are welcome in my home. Come, I'll show you to your bedroom."

Trixie followed him, glancing in all directions, taking everything in. He opened a large door and she felt like she was stepping into a fairy land.

"Is this for real?" she whispered as she gazed at the stunning bedroom.

The windows on the far wall went floor to ceiling like those in the living room. On the opposite wall was the biggest bed she had ever seen covered in what looked like silk blankets and pillows the color of a soft Golden Retriever puppy. She had slipped her shoes off when she entered his home and now she wiggled her bare toes down into the thick white carpet. The tall man led her toward another door and swinging it open he stepped aside as she entered the bathroom. White marble and gold glittered everywhere. She was wondering if the gold was real but was afraid to ask. Next, he showed her a closet, larger than her bedroom at home, with a couple shirts and pairs of jeans and drawers holding a few underthings.

He said, "I did the best I could trying to get some things I hope will fit. Make yourself at home. Are you hungry?"

She glanced up at him, tears shimmering in her magnificent golden eyes. "I'm always hungry." Pausing, she swallowed hard and rushed on. "Why are you doing this for me?"

She watched as a shadow passed over his face. "I'll explain later. Take a shower or a bath and take as long as you like. I'm going to shower and then fix us something to eat." He pointed to her and continued, saying, "When you remove what you are wearing place it outside of your door so I can throw them away." He turned and left.

She stood for a few moments pondering the turn of events in her life. She was in the most beautiful home she had ever seen, with a very handsome man. They were alone. Just the two of them but she felt safer with him than she had felt in months. He had had the chance to rape her but instead had saved her. She started to cry. Big fat tears rolled uncontrolled down her cheeks. What would happen now she wondered as she slipped off every disgusting piece of clothes and dumped them outside the door in the hallway. She made her way to the bathroom and was soon soaking in the largest bathtub she had ever been in. She scrubbed and scrubbed until her golden skin gleamed pink but still she didn't feel clean. She doubted she would ever feel clean again.

Jon was surprised when she entered the kitchen. She looked like the fresh-faced girl he knew she was, her golden skin glowed with all the makeup washed from her face exposing freckles sprinkled across her nose and soft full lips which smiled at him showing even white teeth. He also noticed a fading bruise on her left cheek.

"What happened?" he demanded, and she knew he was asking about the bruise.

"Nothing really."

He said with understanding, "If you ever need to talk, I'll listen."

Offering no acknowledgement of Jon's offer to listen, she made her way to a bar stool, at the kitchen island, and waited as he placed a bowl of soup and crackers in front of her, he apologized, "Sorry, but I usually eat out or order delivery, so, I had to make do with what I had."

"This is fine. Thank you."

After they ate, Jon told her to go pack what he had bought her because he was afraid of staying in the city. He knew they could find him. As they exited the elevator a man stepped from the shadows.

"Hello, Trixie. I saw you walk past me a block away from here and wondered where you was going. You tryin to run away?"

She gasped as Jon stepped in front of her.

The tall lean man with long stringy hair sneered showing black rotting teeth. He chuckled as he glanced at Jon asking, "Who are you and what do you want with her?"

Jon answered with steely calm sending a shiver of fear up Trixie's spine, "I like her and wanted her all to myself."

The man laughed. "Well, you coulda bought her from the pimp, but now you just gonna die and I'm gonna keep her for myself."

Trixie screamed, covering her ears, as she instinctively drew away from Jon, when the roar of gunfire exploded next to her. To her distress she watched Jon holster his handgun and glanced at the man lying dead on the ground.

Before she had a chance to have an emotional breakdown, Jon grabbed her by the arm saying urgently, "Come on, we need to get away from here, now!"

He led her to an underground garage door and once again she was shocked when the door opened to reveal a bright red sports car. Jon helped her into the passenger seat, then quickly jumped into the driver's seat. He carefully backed out and sped away. Trixie glanced at the man driving the car wondering who he was, looking away shyly when he beamed a smile at her. Where was he taking her now? She was so overwhelmed with what was happening to her she couldn't talk. Her mind tumbled in several directions trying to make sense of things. Jon, feeling she must be very confused and wondering about what was happening decided he would tell her a few things and see how she reacted before he told her more.

"Well, I don't think I have ever told you my name." he paused and when she looked at him, he smiled and said, "Hi, my name is Jon Sadler."

She glanced at her lap and whispered, "Hi, Jon, my name is Nicole Richards."

Jon stammered, "But I thought you were Trixie?"

He was surprised to see anger spark in her eyes as she declared vehemently, "I don't ever want to hear that name again! I hate it! The man who killed my parents and kidnapped me told me that was my new name."

Sympathy washed over him. "I'm so sorry, Nicole."

It was wonderful to hear her name again. She asked, "Who are you, Jon Sadler?"

He was pleased she asked her question and replied honestly, "I'm a man who is on a mission and couldn't leave you in that hell hole after I met you."

"What kind of a mission?"

"You asked me why I was doing this so I will tell you the reason why." She waited when he paused sensing she was about to hear a terrible story by the agony on his face. Keeping his eyes on the road he began. "My little brother was 17 years younger than me. He was only 17years old." Nicole noticed he was talking about his brother in the past tense. "His name was Reggie...Reginald Xavier Sadler. After all those people disappeared, he wanted to go with my father and me to the office." Again, he stopped talking and again Nicole waited. She was beginning to think he had changed his mind when he began speaking softly with great sorrow. "We all drove into Seattle, to the office building, and he was kidnapped that day. I tried to save him, but I failed. I tried to find him, but I failed. They murdered him when my father wouldn't pay the ransom." He finally glanced at her his eyes shimmering with emotion. "I couldn't let them destroy you too, Nicole. I had to save you."

She was at a loss for words. What did a person say to someone who had just saved your life? She whispered, "Thank you, Jon." When he glanced at her, she continued. "I'm so sorry about your little brother, and your wife and little boy."

Jon was surprised she had remembered his lie. "I need to tell you the truth. That first night I met you I was trying to think fast and that was the first excuse I came up with." He glanced at her noticing her confusion. "I have never been married and have never had children, but thanks for remembering."

"I can understand why you lied. I'm glad you didn't lose them too."

Jon, changing the subject, asked, "Tell me the truth, Nicole. How old are you?"

She couldn't lie to him. If he despised her for what she was and what she had done she would have to deal with it. "I'm fifteen."

"Only fifteen," Jon was shocked. "I knew you were just a child. I'm old enough to be your father," Jon stated in startled surprise. "Wow! That makes me feel old."

He was serious and Nicole was tickled with his reaction, and she laughed like soft rain tinkling against crystal. She couldn't be offended he thought she was a child, he didn't know she had left her childhood in the past, the day she watched her parents being murdered.

Next, she asked, "Jon, where are we going?"

"To my log cabin in the Cascades. It will be harder to find us there. We'll stay there until I can make arrangements to get you to my parents."

She felt a twinge of panic. "You are going to make me leave you?"

"You'll love my mom and sisters. Trust me."

She still had more she wanted to know. Remembering that apartment he had taken her too and this car she was riding in she asked, "Who are you, Jon? Are you a millionaire or something? What kind of car is this?"

"Well, you have a lot of questions young lady," He laughed. "Ok, I'll answer them. I'm Jon Sadler, CEO of Prism Technologies and son of Amos Sadler, owner and founder of Prism Technologies." He paused glancing at her, enjoying the shock and disbelief on her face.

"Really?" She believed him, which meant his father was one of the richest men in the world.

"Yes, really, and I do have a little money."

"You left out what kind of car is this."

He laughed loudly. "A Ferrari."

She rubbed the seat she was sitting in, glancing around the interior as she whispered in awe, "I'm riding in a Ferrari?"

"Yep! You sure are and maybe if you are a good girl, I might even let you drive it one day."

Nicole zeroed in on one thing he said, 'one day.' He wasn't planning on getting rid of her. Her heart soared. He was her hero. "Really, Jon?"

"Yes, really."

He slowed the car to exit the interstate. They drove another hour neither saying much, Nicole trying to come to terms with her new circumstances, while Jon kicked around several plans in his mind. He slowed and she watched him push a button on the dash, her eyes wide with amazed silence as two huge iron gates swung open. He drove through the gate pushing the button again and she swung around to look out the back window to watch the gates swing shut. As she turned around to gaze into the thick forest blocking her view of everything, she smiled at him. Jon was struck again by how young she truly was, she had been forced to become a woman in many ways, but at this moment she was taking it all in like a bright-eyed child filled with excitement. He rounded the next curve, and his small log cabin came into view. He felt the calm relief that always came over him when he arrived home, because he thought of this little cabin as home. This was the real Jon Sadler not the CEO who helped his father rule the Sadler empire. Nicole was surprised by the simple little cabin but with her acute sense for reading people's emotions she watched Jon visibly relax and saw the lines of worry and anger fade from his face. He loved it here, she realized. He pulled the car around back and parked under the carport which was tucked under the trees growing tall and thick around the cabin barely allowing any sunlight to filter through the thick dark branches. When she stepped from the car and out from under the carport, she realized the forest was so thick it must be impossible to see the cabin and outbuildings from the sky. He was very nicely hidden here.

Jon watched her stop and glance toward the sky, wondering what she was thinking when she said, "I bet no one can see you down here from up there." She pointed to the tree canopy.

Jon was amazed at her perception and grinned at her saying, "That's the whole idea."

She returned his smile, "I like that no one can see us. Makes me feel safe."

When she said that, Jon told her, "That is why we cannot use any phone or internet service up here. It will alert them I'm home."

"Alert who?" Nicole wanted to know.

"The same evil men that run the world and kidnapped you." He said as he led her toward the cabin. "But don't worry, Nicole, they'll never find you again. I promise to keep you safe."

He was concerned when he saw the doubt in her eyes. She didn't trust him. Why? he wondered. He stopped when he stepped on the porch and gazed into her eyes.

"You don't trust me, do you?" He watched a single tear slide down her cheek.

She turned her back to him not wanting to look at him as she whispered, "But what about Reggie?"

Jon felt the knife of her fear stab his heart. Hardening his heart, he answered her question. "You are right. I couldn't protect Reggie, but it was the day after the disappearances and things were crazy and insane and I didn't know how to find him."

"They took me the day after too," she whispered in agony.

Jon forgot his breaking heart, and wrapped the hurting child in his embrace, shocked when a father's love started to bloom in his heart. He placed his large hand under her chin gently turning her tear-stained face up so he could gaze into her eyes as he said, "Nicole, I cannot explain why I care so much for you, but I promise I will keep you safe."

Nicole didn't know if she could ever trust anyone again, she stepped away from him not wanting the human contact as it made her cringe inside, hoping he would be able to protect her, but having serious doubts.

Jon was disappointed when she drew away from him, saying nothing, knowing she had been through hell, he would give her as much time and space as she needed to recover. He was wise enough to realize he needed to get her to his mother as soon as possible. His mother could heal a broken heart and mend a shattered spirit.

CHAPTER 16

Jon unlocked the cabin door allowing her to enter first. The interior was very basic, even though those basics were the best money could buy. She walked into the middle of the ground floor twirling slowly to take in everything. She could tell a woman had probably never been in the cabin because the furniture was plain but sturdy, and there were no decorations of any kind. The kitchen was small and efficient. A huge fireplace dominated the wall opposite the kitchen with a chimney that was made from smooth river stones of various sizes that extended all the way to the second story roof. She noticed a balcony on the second floor extending from the stairs to the outer wall made of rough-hewn logs. The first floor consisted of the living room, eat in kitchen and a bathroom. Jon told her to follow him upstairs and he showed her his large master bedroom then a second bedroom with its own private bathroom which was to be her room. A double sized four poster bed sat in the center of the room covered with a multi-colored hand quilted bedspread and a large dresser hugged the only other wall in the room. Curtains which matched the bedspread hung from the two windows in the room. Jon turned to leave saying he was going to get their suitcases. When he was gone she couldn't resist, she ran and jumped into the middle of the bed, sinking into the softest mattress she had ever lain on. Jon found her rolling around on the bed.

She jumped to the floor when she heard him enter the room and said sheepishly, "The bed is very comfortable."

"So, it would appear," Jon said seriously, trying very hard to contain his laughter.

When she glanced up at him with annoyance, he couldn't help it, he laughed out loud.

"What's so funny?" she demanded.

"You are. Rolling all around the bed like a puppy."

She flopped back on the bed laughing with him, declaring, "It feels like heaven."

He was happy to hear her laughing as he set her suitcase down. "In a few days, when I determine it is safe, we'll go shopping so you can get some more suitable clothes."

She sat up looking at him seriously. "The clothes you got me are fine."

"Yeah, I guess so, but I want you to pick out some things for yourself."

"Thanks Jon, that'll be nice," she answered shyly. She just couldn't understand why he was doing all this for her. He didn't even know her, and she was feeling a little uncomfortable with the kindness he was showing her.

After dinner, later that evening, Jon taught her to play Rummy while they talked about insignificant things. Jon was trying to decide how he was going to approach her with the questions he wanted to ask. He needed to discover what she might know, not wanting to push her, but he didn't have time to waste. He had to find those involved with Reggie's murder and she might have information that could help.

After the game he asked, "Nicole, can we talk?"

Nicole felt her walls go up. She instinctively knew he was going to ask her something uncomfortable, so she was not surprised when he asked, "Can I ask you a few questions?"

He watched her withdraw into herself and feeling frustrated, he pleaded, "Please, Nicole, I need your help."

Not wanting to answer his question, she asked her own, "How can I possibly help you?"

"I think you might have heard something that can help me track down Reggie's murderer."

Nicole was taken aback. She had expected him to ask her something about what she had been through. Jon sat patiently waiting as he watched several emotions play across her face.

She finally glanced at him with curiosity. "I'll try."

He breathed a sigh of relief, saying, "Thanks, Nicole. If I ask something you don't want to answer just say so. Ok?"

"Ok."

He began, "Like I told you, my brother was kidnapped. Did you ever hear of anyone talking about kidnapping a rich kid?"

Nicole thought back to the first few days she had been forced to work at the brothel in Seattle. She replayed conversations she had overheard and suddenly glanced up at Jon in shocked surprise. "I do remember something, Jon. Two slime balls came in when I had been there about a week laughing and bragging about some rich brat they had kidnapped, and they were going to be millionaires."

She paused and Jon could tell she was trying very hard to recall her memories, so he waited patiently.

"Then I didn't see them for a few days, and the next time they came in they started to brag to anyone who would listen that some guy called Nimrod had paid them two million for the boy. I remember feeling sick to my stomach wondering about what was going to happen to him because I thought he was a little boy."

Jon interjected, "Nimrod? Someone named Nimrod?"

"Yes, Jon. I'm sure they said Nimrod."

"That's a strange name. Go on. Can you remember anything else?"

She thought for a few more minutes and shook her head. "I'm sorry, Jon. That's it." He told her she had done great, thrilled he now had a name. He would get her settled with his family at the bunker and return to get serious about his search.

They went to bed after a few more games of Rummy and Jon passed out quickly. He always slept well when he was at his cabin.

He had no idea what time he was awakened by a scream. He came awake, heart pounding, wondering what was happening. He suddenly remembered Nicole and ran to her room finding her whimpering in her sleep and his blood ran cold when she screamed again. He rushed to her side and sat on the bed beside her, gently shaking her until she slowly woke up, eyes wide with fear and breathing rapidly; she curled up in the corner near the wall as far away from him as she could get. When her eyes finally focused on him, she flung herself into his arms.

He held her close, whispering, "It's ok. I'm here. No one can hurt you now."

Nicole clung to Jon feeling safe in his arms, having serious doubts she would ever recover from the kidnapping and forced prostitution. Jon felt his heart breaking for the girl who was shaking in his arms. He was overcome with the sudden need to protect her at all costs.

She finally released her hold of him, saying, "I'm ok now."

He felt her pushing him away emotionally and stood up. "Good night, Nicole."

"Night." she dismissed him, as she snuggled back under the quilt.

He glanced back at her before closing the door, thinking, so this is what it feels like to be a parent. The rest of the night was uneventful.

Over the next few days, they took long hikes through the forest and learned a little more about each other. Her father had died protecting his wife and daughter and her mother had died trying to protect Nicole. Jon discovered she had been an only child, her mother had been white, her father African American, he didn't tell her, but he wondered if that was one of the reasons they had been murdered. He was discovering that the evil in the world knew no limits.

He knew she was a beautiful young lady who was fighting hard to deal with what had happened to her. He never pushed her with questions, he just listened and responded to what she told him.

A week later Jon finally decided they would be safe venturing out and drove into the nearest town. He was surprised to find the small town operating as if the world had not suffered a catastrophe, and it was rather startling after the chaos and riots in Seattle. He found a clothing store and they entered together.

He was delighted when the sales lady said, "Hello, are you here to buy your gorgeous daughter something beautiful to wear?"

Jon smiled at Nicole, telling the woman, "Yes, we are, and I want her to have a good time. Let her have a look around and pick out what she wants."

Jon usually got annoyed with salespeople who gushed over him, but today he kept his thoughts to himself wanting Nicole to enjoy herself as the woman gave Nicole her undivided attention. He had driven the Jeep, so, Jon guessed she could smell his money the way she was fawning over Nicole. Over the next two hours Nicole must have tried on everything in the store. After she picked out a couple shirts and jeans saying that would do, Jon told her that was not enough, and he was serious about her getting what she wanted. So, Nicole did just that. It had been difficult, but she made herself stop looking at the price tags because every time she did Jon demanded, "Nope, don't do that, Nicole."

Jon, sensing the salesclerk was growing suspicious of him buying Nicole everything from undergarments to shoes and socks, said with all the charm he could muster. "I'm just so glad to have my baby girl back. Her mother had her overseas for a year and I didn't get to see her, and when the disappearances happened, they rushed back to America with only the clothes on their back." He paused and whispered to the woman, "Anyway, I like to spoil her." He knew he had been successful when she tottered over to Nicole and gleefully showed her some dainty undergarments.

If there had been any lingering doubts in the woman's mind they vanished when Nicole stepped from the dressing room and stopped in front of Jon and twirled. His eyes lit up with love and pride and the woman knew the girl was his daughter because only a father could look at a child like that.

Nicole had picked out a soft chiffon dress that flowed around her body like a cloud. It was the color of a bright orange flower with shades of bright pink and lavender splashed through the material and the colors next to her caramel colored complexion were stunning. She had put on bright orange sandals and long dangling earrings.

Jon gazed at her as he declared, "You're beautiful, honey."

He was afraid to say more thinking the woman might take it the wrong way, because even though he understood why they had kidnapped her, he couldn't understand why they had hidden this beauty under that grotesque makeup. The child was truly stunning.

After she had returned to the dressing room and exchanged the dress for a new pair of jeans and a colorful top she exited saying, "I have everything I need." She giggled as she added, "And want."

Jon asked, "You are getting that dress you just had on, aren't you?"

She smiled playfully. "Yes, Daddy."

Jon glanced at his feet to hide his surprise. The little minx would hear about that statement.

The delighted salesclerk was enjoying ringing up her sale. He fought the urge to laugh when she finally told him the total. Nicole was flabbergasted, she had never seen that much cash in her life, when Jon paid with several 100 dollar bills. She had no idea clothes could cost so much, but she handled herself like a pro, acting like a spoiled rich girl who didn't have a clue or care about how much things cost.

When they were back in the car she burst into nervous laughter. "Jon, are you sure it was ok to spend that much money?"

"Yes, Nicole. I can afford it and I loved buying those things for you."

When they got back to the cabin, Jon called his father's pilot telling him to meet him at Spokane airport the following day at 6 p.m. Nicole felt fear when she overheard him. Had he changed his mind and was he going to get rid of her because he'd spent so much money on her and was angry?

Jon walked into the house from the porch after he had finished the phone call saying, "We have to leave in the morn..." He stopped when he noticed Nicole sitting on the couch sobbing. "What's wrong, sweetheart?"

She managed to say through her tears. "I heard you say you were leaving. What are you going to do with me?"

Jon realized her complete trust would be a long time coming and said gently, "Nicole, look up at me please." She raised her tear-stained face to him and gazed into his eyes as he continued. "Nicole, I'll never abandon you! We are...me and you together...are leaving tomorrow. We have to move on for our own safety. The longer we stay at any of my properties the more it increases the chance we'll be found." He paused as her crying slowed and handed her a tissue. "We're going to the bunker." He had already told her about the bunker.

"Oh, I thought you didn't want me anymore because I bought so many clothes." As a new thought crossed her mind she asked with dread. "We have to move because of me, don't we?"

"Nicole you are worth more than a billion dollars' worth of clothes." He paused for a second, trying to gather his next words together so he wouldn't hurt her feelings, but she must be told. "Nicole, you have to understand something...the man I rescued you from is very angry you were taken from him and is searching hard to find you. He doesn't yet, know who took you that's why we need to get to the bunker. We;ll be safe there." He reached for her, and she went into his arms as the tears started again. "Nicole, you are worth saving! I knew when I decided to save you, he might discover I had taken you and come after us, but you are worth it. I'm smarter than he is, and I will win, and we'll be safe." Jon wasn't sure he would win but he had to reassure her. "Do you believe me?"

Nicole desperately wanted to believe him, but she knew who he was going up against and she had her doubts. He was a wickedly evil man who seemed to have tentacles into every part of the underworld. She clung to Jon wishing her nightmare was over, but she had a strange sense it was just beginning and said as much for herself as for him. "I believe you, Jon."

"Good," Jon said, backing away from her. "Let's go pack and go for a short hike because I don't know when we'll get back here."

She stood up, saying with forced happiness. "Ok." And returned to her room to pack.

When she walked back downstairs, Jon smiled at her, and Nicole instantly knew he was up to some mischief, "What?" she asked feeling awkward.

"Ready for that hike?"

"Sure."

She was surprised when they headed toward the carport. "Are we going somewhere?"

"Maybe."

They both climbed into the car and Jon drove back to the hard-surfaced road and stopping the car he climbed out. By now Nicole was worried. What was going on? He bent down and glancing at her through the open door grinned like a fool saying. "If you are going to drive this car you better slide over."

Nicole squealed with delight and slid into the driver's seat as Jon climbed into the passenger seat. He explained the clutch and shifting to her, and they started a slow jerking ride down the road. Jon was amazed at how fast she started to pick up shifting the car and in no time she was driving and shifting without difficulty.

She glanced at him, exclaiming. "Wow!"

Jon suddenly feeling very much like a father, yelled. "Keep your eyes on the road!"

Nicole, laughing out loud with pure joy, did as Jon demanded. When they came to a gas station he directed her to turn around in the parking lot and head back home. She turned with ease and soon was cruising along at 30 miles an hour. "That's fast enough," Jon declared.

Nicole knew she was dreaming! She was driving his little red Ferrari! She didn't want this to ever end. She wanted to take it on the interstate and see how fast she could go, instead she shouted with unimaginable joy, "This is fantastic!"

Jon chuckled nervously. He wasn't sure he was enjoying this being a father figure thing. He directed her to turn into his driveway and with relief he could finally breathe again. When he told her to stop in front of the carport, he watched her gently rub her hands around the steering wheel and at last glance up at him the way Reggie used to and realized she had a case of hero worship just as Reggie had had.

She said breathlessly, "Thank you, Jon! That was the most awesome thing I've ever done!"

"I'm glad you enjoyed it and you did really great." he told her as she bounded up the stairs and into the house. He kept a grin on his face as he parked his Jeep Wrangler in front of the house because he was going to drive it now.

He parked the Ferrari under the carport and patted her on the hood whispering, "Gotta leave you for a while, girl. Hope to see you soon."

CHAPTER 17

The next morning, they packed the jeep and were on the road by 9:00. Jon stopped at the same gas station he had made Nicole turn around in yesterday to fill up the jeep, telling her to stay in the car. He didn't want people to know he had a strange young girl with him as his family was well known in the area.

When the gas tank was full, he walked in telling Jim, the store owner. "Hi."

"Hello, Mr. Sadler. How are you today? I thought that was your red car I saw yesterday."

Jon handed Jim enough to cover the bill and felt fear slither up his spine when Jim added, "A few minutes ago, some friends were in here looking for you. Sent them up the road to your place."

Jon couldn't believe he had been so stupid yesterday, letting her drive the car. He hoped no one else had seen them. He had wanted to make her happy and he realized, even if he hurt her feelings, he must harden his heart to keep her alive. He could no longer make spontaneous decisions without considering the consequences. All his friends knew where he lived, so who was looking for him? Maybe the man who had threatened to kill his family? Or maybe Nicole's pimp had found them.

"Thanks, Jim. Could you do me a big favor?" Jon asked.

"Sure, anything you need."

"If anyone else comes in here asking for me tell them you haven't seen me and please don't tell those guys searching for me, I came by here driving my jeep."

Jon hated seeing the fear cross Jim's face. He was a good man. "Ok, Mr. Sadler. They won't get anything out of me."

Jon slipped a couple hundred's in Jim's hand, saying, "Thanks, for your help." as he turned and exited the store rushing to the jeep. Jumping into the driver's seat he was quickly on his way.

Nicole sensing his unease started to shake. "What's wrong, Jon?" she managed to ask.

"Strangers were in the store asking for directions to my cabin."

She knew it, she just knew it. She would never be able to escape! The monster would always find her. She glanced out her window to hide her tears from Jon. He needed to concentrate on driving, not a crybaby girl.

She felt him grab her hand. "Nicole, they don't know we are driving a jeep."

She couldn't answer him or look at him because her fear was overwhelming her. He let go of her hand when she made no response and continued to silently watch the thick forests roll past them.

After driving for an hour, they topped Snoqualmie Pass and started the descent into the interior of Washington State. When they came to the first city which Jon decided was large enough for them to disappear into and not stand out, he asked. "How about some lunch?"

"Do you think it's safe to stop?"

"Yep. We are far enough ahead of them, and we'll be on my Dad's jet before they catch up with us." Pulling into the parking lot of a small local diner he said, "I'm going to make a quick call before we go inside."

Jon had been thinking, while driving, that he should call Clay to meet him in Spokane for added support and protection.

Nicole was pleasantly surprised when he didn't exit the jeep. He trusted her enough to make the call while she could hear what he was saying.

"Clay? That you Clay? This is Jon again. Are you available to make a little trip on my father's jet?"

He winked at Nicole. "I have precious cargo I need to deliver, and I need the best security guard to help protect it." She blushed.

"Great! can you meet us in Spokane in two days? I'll get my father's jet pilot to pick you up in Roanoke and then you can meet me in Spokane. Thanks again! See you in a couple days."

There, he said it again thought Nicole, 'his father's jet', her amazements kept coming. She barely listened to the end of the conversation still wondering about 'his father's jet'. She could not comprehend anyone so rich they owned their own jet.

A little ripple of pleasure shivered through her when Jon declared, "Well come on, Squirt, I'm starving" as he left the jeep. Squirt, she liked that. No one had ever given her a nickname. Feeling at ease finally, she jumped from the jeep and walked with Jon to the restaurant. He was good at that, she realized, being able to calm her nerves.

As he opened the door for her to enter the restaurant, he whispered, "Just remember to call me Dad."

She grinned widely up at him. "Sure thing, Daddy."

"Think you're cute, don't you?"

She flounced inside without answering, feeling very spunky.

After they had finished lunch Jon stopped by a grocery store and let her pick up a few snacks and when they were once again traveling up I-90 she asked the question that had been eating at her since he had used the phone. "Can I ask you something?"

"Sure," Jon replied, glad she was in a much better mood and talking.

"How come you told me I couldn't use a phone, but you did?"

Leave it up to a kid to ask a question like that, but maybe there was someone she wanted to call. He hadn't thought about that. "The phone I used is a prepaid phone that I use until the minutes are gone, then throw it away and switch to a new one. They can be tracked, but I throw them away after I'm done with them. Makes it almost impossible to find me. When we first got to the cabin, I didn't have any of those phones."

"Really?" Nicole asked in amazement. "You think of everything, don't you?"

Jon chuckled. "I try. Being CEO of Prism Technologies gives me an advantage." He glanced at her. "Nicole, I should've asked before now, but is there anyone you want to call?"

It broke his heart that a 15year old child had been through so much she was smart enough to answer, "No, there is no one. Even if there was, I wouldn't call them and take any chances they might get killed because they had talked to me."

"Well, if you do decide you want to call anyone you can use my phone."

"Thank you," she mumbled and preceded to again silently watch the world go by outside of her car window.

CHAPTER 18

They made it to Spokane and Jon rented a motel room for two nights at a national motel chain. They only ventured from the room to get a hot dinner. Two days later Clay arrived, but Nicole was shyly refusing to talk to anyone. They all climbed into the jet and again Nicole was stunned. So, this was how the rich flew! Her first plane ride and she was flying in a private jet with leather seats and a tiny kitchen stocked with everything Jon wanted. A TV hung on a wall near the back and a cabinet held every kind of electronic equipment one could imagine or need. The pilot introduced himself to Clay and Nicole then entered the cockpit. Jon directed her to a seat, and she sat down making sure the seatbelt was as tight as she could fasten it.

Jon noticed Nicole gripping the armrests of her seat so tightly her knuckles were turning white.

"Nicole, have you ever flown before?" he asked gently.

She turned eyes wide with fear toward him as she shook her head 'no'.

"It'll be ok. We have the best pilot flying for us."

She still made no reply. Jon tried again. "Would you like to watch a movie?"

She shook her head again. He noticed she kept darting fearful glances at Clay also. Jon had no idea how to help calm her fears or settle her nerves.

The plane slowly taxied to the runway and Nicole's face turned ashen when the jet engines roared to life and the plane started to speed ever faster down the runway.

Jon decided, maybe if she saw his excitement, it might help her cope. "Here we go, Nicole! In a minute we will lift off from the ground and be air-borne. I love that feeling, Nicole. We'll be floating in the air."

Nicole felt like she was going to be sick, and Jon's enthusiasm wasn't helping any. Then to her surprise she felt it just like Jon had said. The moment the wheels left the earth. The magic moment she was floating.

Jon watched the change come over her face and said, "Look out the window, Nicole. Watch everything get smaller as we lift higher."

She did as he directed and watched the world below start to look like toys. The cars and buildings shrinking smaller and smaller. "It's magical Jon."

"Yeah, I know. I love to fly!"

Clay had his footrest up and appeared to be napping, but Nicole still cast wary glances his way. When she was sure he was sleeping and posed no threat to her she watched the world below speed by. She was learning very quickly to like flying and wished she never had to return to the earth below where dangers seemed to lurk everywhere.

In a few hours they had landed in Roanoke and Jon quickly rented a car after he had made another phone call. He drove to where the bunker fence gate used to be and stopped in the middle of nowhere. Nicole was very nervous and afraid when another car drove up and stopped beside the parked rental car. She broke out in a cold sweat and fought the urge to throw up as she started to visibly shake when two more strange men walked up to Jon. What was going to happen to her? She wondered. Had it all been a lie and was she being sold to new monsters?

"Thanks again, Fred," Jon said cheerfully and handed him the phone he had been using saying, "Get rid of this for me, somewhere in Roanoke."

Grabbing the phone, Fred replied, "Sure boss, anytime." He would drop the phone into the Roanoke River an hour later.

The one named Fred climbed into the rental car, turned it around and headed back to Roanoke as the other man followed him in the car they had arrived in, leaving Clay, Jon and Nicole standing alone. Nicole was thoroughly confused and terrified.

"Come on, we have a little walk. Just a couple of miles," Jon declared seemingly oblivious to Nicole's discomfort; but he was not, he knew they had to get off the road and into the forest at once. He didn't have time to comfort her or encourage any hysterics. She would just have to cope and trust him.

Clay carried his backpack while Jon and Nicole each carried one of her suitcases and set off into the forest. Nicole did notice how beautiful the mountain forest was but just couldn't enjoy it because of her increasing anxiety. Suddenly, Jon stopped in front of a small hill surrounded by mountain cliffs and started to push his way through the thick forest undergrowth. She was shocked when Jon caused a hidden door to slide open.

Now that they had made it safely to the bunker Jon turned to smile reassuringly at Nicole. "We're finally at the bunker, Nicole."

They silently followed Jon into a tunnel which brought them to the main living area where they were met by Jon's family. Jon had not lied to her, thought Nicole, there really was a bunker with his family living here.

Nicole was greeted first by a gray-haired lady with gentle blue eyes who smiled sweetly saying softly, "So you must be Nicole. Welcome, sweetheart. I'm Jon's mother, Betty."

Nicole was surprised when she instantly felt calm relief flow through her at the soft-spoken words of Betty. Her words seemed to offer comfort and peace.

"Hello," Nicole replied shyly.

Jon introduced the rest of his family to Nicole. Unknown to Nicole, Jon had told his mother all he knew about the girl, knowing his mother would be discreet and not bring up the past to Nicole, but she needed to be aware, to know how to help the child recover.

The next day Jon left, and Nicole found herself uncomfortably alone with these complete strangers. They reintroduced themselves and Katie smiled at her asking, "Do you like horses, Nicole?"

"Horses?" Nicole asked.

"Yeah, I was wondering because we have two of them that need to be taken outside today and thought you might like to help with them."

Nicole's eyes lit up with delight. "I would love that! I've ridden my whole life."

Katie led Nicole into the meadow, and they began their leisurely ride around the perimeter along the wood line. They rode along in silence until Nicole asked, "Why did your brother do this for me? Rescue me and bring me here?"

Katie glanced over at the troubled teen and spoke softly. "I'm not really sure, Nicole. He can be a very hard man who will not bend, but there is a gentleness to him he likes to keep hidden. He was always rescuing me and Chloe when we were kids. Maybe he just wanted to rescue you."

"That's what he told me but it's so hard to believe he wanted to rescue someone he doesn't even know."

"Jon is an excellent judge of character and I think he saw something in you worth saving." Katie smiled reassuringly at Nicole who glanced away shyly.

Healing and believing would take time Katie realized. "Well, come on, I'll race you back to the bunker." she challenged Nicole and was caught off guard when Nicole kicked her horse into action and took off first. Katie laughed and immediately gave chase.

They pulled their horses to a stop, laughing, in front of a waiting Clay who asked, "So, who won?"

"I did!" they both declared simultaneously, as Katie jumped to the ground first. Nicole noticed the way Clay and Katie glanced at each other realizing they were more than just friends. She wondered if they were aware of their feelings.

The girls grabbed the reins of their horses and the three of them made a few short laps cooling the horses before they reentered the bunker, Nicole saying, "I'll brush the horses."

"That's not necessary," Katie said.

"Really, I'll do it. I love to brush them."

Realizing Nicole needed some time alone, Katie said, "Ok, see you upstairs."

Nicole silently brushed the horses enjoying the solitude. She was overwhelmed by the turn of events in her life, amazed she was in this place with a group of strangers brushing horses. She leaned forward placing her forehead against the horse's warm side as the tears streamed down her face, whispering, "Mom, Dad, I miss you!" as a great wave of despair and sadness washed over her.

Nicole forced herself to stop crying and when she had finished, she made her way upstairs to find most of the family involved in a game of Rummy. Mr. Sadler sat off to himself reading a book while Mrs. Sadler sat on the couch knitting.

She glanced up at Nicole and patted the couch seat beside her. "Come, visit with me." she said softly.

Nicole shyly glanced at the people around her, realizing they were engrossed in their game, not paying any attention to her, so she slowly made her way toward Betty and sat down on the couch beside her.

"What are you doing?" Nicole asked Betty.

"Knitting. Helps me relax," Betty replied. "If you would be interested, I can teach you to knit."

Nicole shook her head, saying, "No, that's ok." She just couldn't imagine knitting being fun.

"What do you like to do?" Betty asked gently.

"Well, I love to ride and take care of the horses. And I love to draw and paint."

Betty smiled brightly causing a shiver of pleasure to ripple through Nicole. "Why, Nicole, that sounds amazing. We have an artist in our presence." She declared to the family.

Katie glanced toward Nicole, saying, "I've been trying to learn how to draw. Maybe you can give me some pointers."

Nicole blushed pink. "Oh, I'm not very good. I just kinda doodle."

"You'll have to show me what you can do, sometime," Betty encouraged her.

"Maybe," Nicole replied shyly.

Betty changed subjects. "What grade are you in?"

"I was in 10th grade, but I guess I won't finish school now that the world has gone crazy."

Betty smiled again. "I bet Art was your favorite class."

Nicole laughed softly, causing Katie to glance at her again, glad her mother was helping Nicole feel safe enough to open up. "Yes, Mrs. Sadler, that was one of my favorites along with FFA."

"FFA?" Betty asked.

"Yeah, Future Farmers of America. I loved it."

The game over, the family sat down to supper and when they were finished Clay, Katie, and Chloe asked Nicole to join them for a walk outside before they had to lock up for the night. She was pleased to be included and the four of them set off for a quick walk.

They had walked about halfway across the meadow when Clay stopped and whispered, "Wait! Someone is coming."

Nicole felt sick with fear when a stranger walked out of the forest and headed toward them, all she could think was she had been found. She was fighting the urge to run away screaming in terror, when Katie asked, "Does anyone recognize him?"

Everyone shook their heads as they silently watched the man walk ever closer toward them. He was of average height with dark hair waving about his head, dressed in jeans and a shirt with a backpack slung over his shoulders. He stopped about 100 feet away and asked, "Is this the Sadler Compound?"

How did he know this they wondered? Clay had just started calling the bunker this about a week ago. He had grown tired of the word bunker.

"Who are you looking for?" Clay demanded.

The man smiled. "You have no need to fear me, Clay." He paused and glanced at the others in the group. "You all have no need to fear me, Chloe, Katie or Nicole. God has sent me."

The women gazed at him in growing fear as Clay lifted his rifle to point it at the man's chest. "Who are you?"

Nicole shocked everyone when she shouted hysterically, "It's me isn't it? He has found me! Please don't hurt them. I'll go with you."

Katie grabbed Nicole holding her close as she cried and the man said calmly, "I didn't mean to frighten you. My name is Aaron and I'm from Israel. I'm one of 144,000 men whom God has sent out into the world to tell people about Him, and He has sent me to your family."

The women gazed at him in disbelief and Clay asked again, still pointing the gun at Aaron's chest. "What do you want?"

Aaron replied calmly, "First, I have not been sent here to bring you back to Nimrod, Nicole."

Nicole asked breathlessly, "Nimrod was the man who tortured me?"

Aaron replied softly, feeling sadness for the pain Nicole had suffered. "Yes, Nicole, it was Nimrod."

Clay said, "If you are looking for Nicole, I think I need to eliminate you so you cannot tell Nimrod how to find her."

"I don't work for Nimrod. God told me to tell Nicole she is safe from Nimrod. He will never find her." Aaron continued to speak calmly.

It was becoming rather creepy thought Katie and Chloe. Nicole's only feelings were hysterical terror, causing her to feel like she was going to pass out.

Aaron continued. "I've been chosen by God to come here to share the good news that God wants you to know the truth about His salvation and about His Son Jesus." He paused and his eyes focused on Chloe. "Chloe, God knows you have asked Him to save you and have many questions which I'm here to help answer for you. God wants you all to understand."

Chloe gasped when Aaron told her this and Katie looked at her quizzically. "What's he talking about, Chloe?"

Chloe answered softly, "Aaron is right. I asked God to save me a few days after Jim and the girls disappeared." She gazed intently at Aaron. "Are they in heaven?"

Aaron smiled radiantly. "Yes, they are."

Chloe started to cry, and Katie hugged her. Clay finally lowered the gun realizing something amazing was taking place that couldn't be explained, because Aaron knew things that only the family could know.

Clay said, "Well, I guess we should welcome you. Would you like to come meet the Sadler's?"

Aaron smiled again and walked up to the group extending his hand toward Clay for a handshake. Clay grabbed his hand. "Nice to meet you, Aaron. Well, it's time we went back to the Sadler's Compound."

The group chuckled, still slightly nervous and followed Clay back inside.

As they entered the living area of the bunker Amos glared at Aaron. "What's going on? Who is this you have allowed to enter the bunker?" he asked irritably.

Betty rushed to their visitor. "Hello, young man."

Aaron replied, "Thank you, Mrs. Sadler, for the warm welcome."

Betty immediately felt concern over the stranger who had entered their home. Where had he come from? He upset her even more when he tried to calm her. "Hello, Betty Sadler. God has heard your questions and I've been sent to help you understand."

She backed away from him as Chloe rushed forward. "Mom, this is Aaron, and he knows I asked God to save me and has come to help me."

Amos roared, "Now we are back to talking about salvation again?"

Aaron spoke serencly. "Amos, I'm here to help you. God has sent me. I mean no harm and I won't intrude for long." He gazed intently at Amos. "May I stay with your family for as long as I am needed?"

Amos felt deflated. How could he argue with this man? He really did seem to have been sent here by God, even though Amos refused to acknowledge there was a God, he felt like God had sent this man.

It was very disturbing, but he mumbled, "Yes, you can stay," and he turned to walk to his room. He needed to be alone to think about this strange turn of events.

CHAPTER 19

Aaron had been at the Sadler Compound for ten days when the first one accepted God's gift of salvation; he was surprised it was Clay. The Marine Warrior knew he desperately needed God's forgiveness and asked Jesus to save him. No matter how many times Aaron witnessed a person reach out to God to save them, it still thrilled him. Next it was Betty's turn. Aaron was now having wonderful, intense Bible studies with Clay, Chloe and Betty as he knew he must leave soon, and he must give them as much knowledge as he could impart. Then the big shocker. He had been having serious doubts Amos would ever get over his bitterness and anger over the loss of his sons, enough to consider accepting God's salvation, but Aaron had just helped Amos come to God. Every person's salvation was a precious gift, but for Aaron, witnessing Amos' salvation would always be a special memory. Watching the disabled man who was being destroyed with bitterness reach out to God had been amazing. Now he had private Bible studies with Amos, because he felt God had special plans for Amos and the Sadler family and was leading Aaron to educate him as thoroughly as possible. Amos proved to be a passionate, quick learner, who was like a sponge soaking up the Bible.

Aaron explained to Amos about what was going to transpire during the Tribulation. The seven years when God was going to pour out His wrath on planet Earth. Amos felt fear creep up his spine when Aaron told him of the apocalyptic earthquakes, and weather, wars, pestilence and demonic creatures from the pit of hell that were about to be unleashed on mankind and according to Aaron it was about to start happening very soon. Amos' first thought was he needed to get Jon back to the bunker.

Aaron had given the Bible verse Proverbs 3:6 to be used as their secret password. He told them he would say "In all thy ways acknowledge Him" and the family would reply with the remainder of the verse, "and He shall direct thy paths." Aaron told them if he ever sent anybody to them, they would use this password as proof they had been sent by him.

Then to Aaron's disappointment he knew it was time to move on and leave Katie and Nicole's salvation in the hands of Jesus and the Sadler family. He had managed to find Nicole alone with the horses about a week before he was going to leave and had attempted to talk with her about what had happened to her. "Nicole, God does love you. He didn't do those things to you. Satan did."

She lashed out. "Why did God allow me to be tortured and raped. I guess you and God know I was raped over and over again, and you say God loves me. I don't believe you!"

She turned from Aaron hiding her angry tears from him. "Leave me alone, Aaron! I will never believe in God!" and she ran up the tunnel away from him as Aaron silently lifted a prayer for God to comfort Nicole.

The day Aaron said good-bye there were many tears, as he reminded them. "I must take the Good News to others. I'll see you again soon, read your Bible, pray and remember God is in charge and loves each of you." Then he set off to follow Gods leading, with excitement over the next people to whom he would witness.

The family watched him walk away until he disappeared into the forest.

REVENGE

CHAPTER 20

When Jon returned to Spokane, he was pleased to see the jeep where he had left it parked. He did a quick sweep to check for damage and hidden tracking devices. The jeep was clean. So far so good. The pimp still must not know who had stolen Nicole from him.

Jon debated what he should do now. Fearing returning to his cabin or his penthouse just yet, with revenge gnawing at his soul, he made a quick decision he should try to contact Agamemnon. He needed his help.

He knew it was about a 15-hour drive to Oakland, so he decided he would drive halfway today and finish tomorrow. Finding it hard to believe Agamemnon had changed as much as Clay insinuated, Jon decided he needed to be rested and alert when he met him again, just in case Clay was right.

Two days later he was in Oakland and had found the location of the warehouse and secured a motel room.

The next evening after dark Jon cautiously made his way toward the door in the large cinderblock warehouse. Pounding on the door, he was rewarded with a harsh voice demanding to know who it was. He gave the secret password and was pleased when the door slowly slid open revealing two large men covered in tattoos holding assault rifles pointed at him.

"Who are you?" one thug demanded.

Jon ignored the question saying, "I'm here to see Agamemnon."

They ushered him inside leading him to a small room. Jon's nerves were on edge, tingling over his entire body, he didn't like the way things were going and couldn't help but remember Clay's warning.

The men glanced at each other before they turned vile grins toward him. "Who is this Agamemnon?"

Jon said between clenched teeth. "You know who he is, and I demand to see him. Tell him Jon Sadler wants to see him."

One of the men chuckled. "Demand to see him?"

The other said, "Hand over your gun and I'll take you to him."

Jon had no idea if Agamemnon was still here and anyway, he had no intention of handing over his gun to anyone. "Sorry, fellas, but the gun stays with me."

The one who wanted his gun glared at him threateningly. "You can leave now, or I'll remove your gun from your dead body."

All three men jumped when a deep gravelly voice boomed over the hidden intercom system. "Idiots! Bring him to me!"

Jon was relieved when he recognized Agamemnon's voice. The men turned quickly, leading him down a dark, dingy hall and into another, larger room. As they entered the room Jon noticed a man lying on his back, upon an exercise bench, grunting with each lift of the massive weights he was working out with. He placed the weights back in the rack above his head and heaved himself into a sitting position with his legs straddling the bench. Jon had not seen Agamemnon since they had been together in Iraq and was again shocked at the sight of the man. He was huge, standing 7ft 5 inches tall and larger than any man Jon had ever known. His large black body glistening with sweat was covered in grotesque tattoos across his chest and arms, while his gleaming bald head reflected the lights in the room. Black eyes the color of wet ink gazed intelligently from his large round face. His nose was wide and flat above large full lips which spread into a grin showing even white teeth when he saw Jon. Large diamond earrings sparkled from each ear lobe and several large gold chains hung from his neck to the middle of his large bare chest. He was large and lean, the muscles rippling across his chest and down his abdomen.

A long pink scar traveled from his left temple down toward his jaw. Jon remembered when he had received that scar in Iraq. They had just arrived at a local village in Iraq when Agamemnon stepped from the Hummer sending the villagers screaming in terror. One brave Iraqi had tried to take a sword to him but only succeeded in cutting him and igniting his rage. The Iraqi's death had been swift.

Agamemnon stood up grabbing a towel and preceded to wipe the sweat from his eyes as he signaled for Jon to come near with a hand that appeared to be as large as an iron frying pan. Jon had seen him kill a man with one punch of those monstrous fists. Jon standing 6ft 2 inches tall suddenly felt dwarfed as Agamemnon towered above him, and he was relieved he was a friend. Jon felt no fear in Agamemnon's presence, just a healthy respect, but at times Jon had wondered to himself if maybe, just maybe, some of those conspiracy theories about aliens abducting people were true and Agamemnon was the product of an alien experiment. Wherever he had come from, Agamemnon was lethal.

Agamemnon spoke, his deep voice vibrating around the room. "Jon, I'm glad to see you." He paused, knowing Jon needed him. "What brings you here?"

Jon replied, "Thanks for seeing me, Agamemnon. I need your help."

"How can I help you?" he asked while he signaled everyone else to leave the room, growling, "Leave us!"

Once the room was empty of all but the two of them, Jon sat in a chair facing him and began. "About two months ago my younger brother was kidnapped and held for ransom. My hard-headed father thought he could browbeat the kidnappers into returning my brother alive and refused to pay the ransom. Three weeks ago, they dumped my brother's body in front of my parents' house. I need help finding them."

Jon was surprised to see compassion briefly flit across Agamemnon's face. "I'm sorry this has happened to your family. I'll help any way I can. Tell me what you know." He hesitated, then asked, "Jon, what do you plan on doing when you find out who is responsible for this?"

"Kill them," Jon replied flatly, anger burning in his blue eyes.

Agamemnon nodded his understanding. "I'll not only help you discover who has done this, but any of my supplies or weapons you may need are at your disposal."

Agamemnon continued, knowing Jon would probably not like what he was going to say. "I wish you to stay with me for a few weeks, Jon."

Jon was surprised. "Why?"

"You're not ready to enter my world."

Agamemnon was not disappointed when Jon glared at him, those ice blue eyes burning with rage. "Yes, I am!" he hissed.

Agamemnon replied calmly, "I can see you are in great shape, but you need more than a six-pack, Jon." Taking a breath, he picked his words carefully. "I can put you through a training program that will give you the skills to survive in my world where only the fittest survive. You must learn to be ruthless, Jon."

"Doesn't Iraq count?" Jon asked curtly, trying to control his anger.

Agamemnon shook his head slowly. "Iraq was child's play compared to the world you are about to enter."

Jon's anger cooled when he remembered his trips to Seattle's Underground City and knew Agamemnon was right. Resigning himself to the inevitable, he whispered, "Ok."

Agamemnon smiled. "Good! You start in the morning."

As he stood up, Jon said, "I'm worried the longer I delay the harder it will be to find out who murdered Reggie."

"Do not worry. I'll start my own investigation." He paused, black eyes glaring intensely at Jon, who felt a twinge of fear. "My men will search, and no one will be aware they are searching. They'll get answers for you without giving you away."

Jon nodded his agreement.

"We'll leave now and go to my compound," he said standing up. "Come with me."

Agamemnon made his way down another hallway and out a door which led to a waiting SUV limo.

"My jeep is parked at a parking garage a few blocks over. I can get it and follow you," Jon said, desperately not wanting to get in the limo.

Agamemnon stopped and turned to face Jon. "The choice is yours to make, Jon. Go with me now or go your own way."

Jon silently entered the limo as yet again he felt a twinge of fear when one of Agamemnon's private security guards crawled in and sat next to Jon holding a 44-magnum handgun. What was he getting himself into? Agamemnon gazed silently at Jon watching him fight the urge to squirm and slowly a smile twitched the large man's lips.

"Relax, Jon. You're among friends," Agamemnon said too smoothly for Jon's comfort as he glanced sideways at the thug holding the gun.

Agamemnon chuckled. "He has nothing to do with you. I never travel without him."

Jon didn't believe him. He knew if he twitched the wrong way, he would be dead before he could draw his own gun.

Agamemnon continued. "If I did not trust you, I would've removed your weapons from you."

Jon felt slight relief. "I was wondering."

Agamemnon laughed. "I bet you were."

Jon chuckled awkwardly.

Agamemnon said, "While we drive to the house, I want you to tell me what you know."

Jon relaxed a little and told him about Reggie's kidnapping, going to the underground city, rescuing Nicole and that she thought someone named Nimrod might have kidnapped Reggie.

Agamemnon glanced away from Jon, to hide his surprise, knowing he was now going to use him. He would help Jon, but he would also use him. He had been waiting for such an opportunity. The man called Nimrod was a thorn in his side and he wanted him eliminated and Jon was going to do just that for him. He was stunned to find out it had been Jon who had turned Nimrod's world temporarily upside down when he had stolen the girl right out from under Nimrod's nose. The man had raged with anger, killing all who had been in charge of the girls. He doubted Nimrod was aware it was Jon who had done this because if he knew, Agamemnon could almost guarantee he would have employed every crime syndicate in the world to hunt him down. Agamemnon had no intention of letting Jon know any of this, he would discover how to confront Nimrod soon enough, right now he needed to make sure Jon was prepared to survive.

CHAPTER 21

Jon was astonished when they entered Agamemnon's compound. A very large mansion dominated the hilltop with several large outbuildings. The limo stopped at one of those outbuildings and the three passengers stepped out of the car. Jon stood silently looking around him at the immaculate lawns, thinking Agamemnon was doing well for himself. Agamemnon directed Jon to follow him as they entered the building and introduced him to Rex, a grotesquely muscled and tattooed man who was much shorter than Jon. The man never smiled or offered a handshake, just glared silently at Jon as Agamemnon gave the man instructions about training him. Jon stood stoically glaring at the man itching to have his chance to fight him, as he had no doubts about his ability to put the ugly little man in his place.

Agamemnon turned toward Jon saying, "Rex will show you to the room you'll use as long as you are here and talk with you about the schedule he will make for you. You're not to come near the mansion, and I'll call for you if I need to talk with you." He paused smiling wickedly at Jon. "Have fun and try to survive."

Jon wanted to ask how he was going to contact Agamemnon if he wanted to leave but would not give him that satisfaction and kept his mouth shut. Once again, he wondered what he was getting himself into. The repulsive man Rex led him to a small bedroom and said in a raspy voice for Jon to meet him back in the gym in 20 minutes. Jon took in the sparse, cramped, musty room which housed one twin bed, straight back chair and nothing else. Not even a window. He suddenly felt like he was in jail. He left to return to the gym realizing he might as well get started with his survival training, he thought contemptuously, still feeling Agamemnon was exaggerating his need for improvement.

He entered the gym and Rex stopped his workout with the punching bag asking flatly, "You ready?"

"Might as well be. Nothing else to do."

Rex pointed to a locker room door. "Go change into some workout clothes. There are several closets and you should be able to find something."

Jon was pleased to find the locker room and clothing clean. He quickly changed and was back in the gym watching Rex throw punches at the punching bag. Suddenly, Rex swung around to face him and before Jon could even react Rex's fist connected with Jon's jaw sending him flying backwards, causing him to flip over a treadmill. Jon was swiftly back on his feet as Rex smiled contemptuously at him.

"What's your problem?" Jon demanded rubbing his aching jaw.

Rex stated seriously. "You want to live? You must always be alert." Then to goad him more. "I thought you was a marine who fought in Iraq."

Rex was pleased to watch Jon's eyes grow ice cold, and hatred flare. Jon started to walk lithely like a big cat stalking its prey as he circled Rex looking for a chink in his defense. Rex stood tense, muscles taut, waiting anxiously to see what the big man had in him.

When Jon made his move, attempting to ram his fist in Rex's side, he was met with a lightning fast elbow to his sternum which made him double over, his face slamming into Rex's large beefy fist as he brought it up under Jon's chin jarring his teeth as his mouth slammed shut. Rex watched as Jon crumpled to the floor at his feet, knocked out cold. Rex shook his head in disappointment hoping he would be able to get this man fit enough to keep himself alive. The only thing Jon had going for him was that he had been a marine and could train hard.

Rex reached for a pitcher of water and poured it in Jon's face. Jon sat up spitting and sputtering wiping the water out of his eyes as he looked around in stunned silence until his eyes found Rex. Rex stretched forth his hand offering Jon a hand up, but Jon jumped to his feet landing a punch in Rex's stomach which surprised him with its strength. Rex grunted with the impact but remained upright on his feet as he swung his right leg up attempting to kick Jon in his groin, but Jon jumped out of the way as he grabbed a chair and cracked it over Rex's head, springing back out of his reach, as Rex buckled to the floor, rubbing his head, searching for any bleeding.

Rex grabbed a broken chair leg. Jumping to his feet, he circled Jon swinging the chair leg in an infinity pattern in front of him protecting his mid-section. Rex's eyes locked onto Jon's furious gaze waiting for the perfect moment. Like the predator he was, he would be fully aware when Jon's intense anger waned even a fraction. There it was! Rex swung the chair leg with lightning speed hitting Jon hard across his back, but to his astonishment he realized Jon was a predator too when he grabbed Rex around the neck with his long and powerful arms, locking them in a death grip as he started to strangle him. Rex realized he couldn't pry Jon loose. He elbowed Jon in the ribs, discovering Jon was in an angered frenzy and was oblivious to any pain Rex inflicted. The harder he struggled the tighter Jon's choke hold became, until Rex started to feel light-headed. Frantically, Rex remembered he still held the chair leg and swung it around slamming it with all his strength at Jon's head hitting him in the forehead; the skin split open like a ripe watermelon sending blood splattering over the two of them. Jon let go as they both sank to the floor, Jon trying to stop the blood running down his face while Rex sucked in air.

When Rex could finally breathe, he said, "I will not fight you any more today. Come with me and we'll take care of your head."

Jon could barely see him through the blood running into his eyes and even though he didn't want to trust the man he knew he needed help. Getting to his feet he followed Rex into a medical room and took the seat Rex indicated.

Rex removed some medical supplies from a cabinet handing Jon a bottle of whiskey. "You're going to need a swig of this."

Jon glanced at him with trepidation wondering what was about to happen.

"Lean your head back and cover your eyes," Rex demanded handing Jon a clean towel.

Jon did as he was told and suddenly jerked back into an upright position, yelling, "What's wrong with you? Jerk!" Rex had poured the whiskey into the gash on his forehead.

Rex ignored Jon's anger. "Don't want any infection. Lay your head back and let me sew you up."

Jon glared at him with hatred, realizing he was going to sew up the gash on his head without any numbing medication, he grabbed the bottle from Rex and took a much larger gulp splashing some of the liquid down the front of Rex when he shoved the bottle back at him, then he lay back in the reclining chair determined not to make a sound.

Jon clenched his teeth together determined not to cry out with the excruciating pain that surged through him when Rex pushed the needle through the skin on his scalp. Rex was going to pay for this, Jon promised himself. After the third stitch the pain eased, Jon not sure if it was the whiskey or his body numbing itself against the pain, he was just relieved.

Rex was done in a few minutes and Jon sat up glaring daggers at him. Rex stepped away from him saying, "We'll take it easy a couple days to give that cut a chance to heal. I still have much I can teach you. Come on, I'll show you the kitchen."

Jon followed the grotesque little man, reluctantly admitting to himself he was a formidable adversary. Maybe Agamemnon was correct, and he could learn from Rex.

CHAPTER 22

The next three weeks Jon developed a grudging respect for Rex. The little man was the best teacher Jon had ever had, even better than the Marines. The Marines had taught him how to survive combat, Rex was teaching him to survive in a world full of predators whose one goal was to kill him. Rex honed Jon's senses until he was hyper aware of the world around him, showing him the many ways he was vulnerable to attack.

Jon wondered why he didn't have his own gym but refused to pry. Today, Rex had one more lesson to teach Jon. He was pleased with Jon's progress but needed to give him a real-life lesson. He excused himself and left the building by a back door, Jon knew nothing about, while Jon worked out with the punching bag.

Jon methodically punched the bag but stopped when a shiver of warning slithered up his spine. He glanced around the gym and noticed two men watching him across the gym near the entrance. He silently watched them, wondering what they wanted when one asked, "You Jon?"

Jon's stomach did a flip as he did a sweep of the room, wondering where Rex was. How did these men come to be here? So much for Agamemnon's promises of anonymity, his spies hadn't done so well.

"Maybe," Jon answered evasively.

Jon watched the men separate and walk around the boxing ring heading toward him, blocking his ability to escape. His defenses kicked into overdrive, as a trickle of sweat rolled down his spine, "What do you want?" Jon demanded.

"To make you pay for Nicole."

The mention of Nicole's name should have warned Jon, but he was giving his full concentration to the men and missed the slip. They had called her by her given name, not Trixie, Agamemnon was the only person in the compound who knew her true identity, because Jon had told him.

Jon did a quick sweep of the gym still not seeing Rex and realized he was going to have to face them alone. Making a quick assessment he decided the man to his right should be the one he engaged first, but they had their own plans. He started to slowly advance on them when they rushed him at the same time. He was ready. Rex had taught him well. He acted like he was going to attack the man on his left but did a 360 degree turn kicking the one on his right in the gut as he grabbed a chair and swung it toward the other man grazing him on the shoulder, then jumped out of reach, feeling intense pain when he was struck hard across his back with what felt like a ton of bricks. He crumpled to the floor as the wind whooshed from his lungs, taking deep breaths giving himself time to recover, he listened to his tormentors laugh at how quickly they had defeated him. Harnessing the anger burning in his soul Jon slowly rose to his hands and knees, pausing to give them a false sense of security that they had won. Springing to his feet Jon kicked one in the gut sending him flying backwards striking his head on the cinder block wall, while he grabbed the other man shoving him into the ropes around the boxing ring winding the ropes around the man's head, causing the rope to twist tightly around the man's throat choking him. As he choked the man, he brought his elbow down with all his strength hitting him in the middle of his back with his elbow. The man crumpled at the side of the boxing ring with his head still caught in the ropes and Jon left him lying there, hoping he would choke to death. He went to finish off his other attacker. The man was struggling to his feet wiping the blood away from the gash on the back of his head, glancing at Jon when he heard his footsteps approaching, silently he watched Jon advance toward him. Jon stopped, out of the other man's reach, glaring at him with intense hatred waiting patiently for the man to move. Hearing a moan from the man tangled in the ropes caused the bleeding attacker to glance toward his accomplice, then he started to slowly advance toward Jon suddenly whipping a switch blade knife open, and with lightning fast speed he swung the knife at him as Jon used his arm to protect his face feeling the burning fire as the razor-sharp knife sliced his right forearm.

"STOP!" Rex yelled.

The hand holding the knife dropped to the man's side. Jon catching a glimpse of movement, backed away from his assailant, noticing Rex untangling the choking man.

Rex growled, "You were instructed not to harm him!"

Jon gazed at the men around him realizing he had been set up, rage settling on him. "So, this was a set up?! I'm done!" and he turned to stomp out of the gym.

Rex said calmly, "How else will you learn?"

Jon stopped, his icy cold eyes finding Rex. "You call this a lesson?" he demanded swinging his bleeding arm up in front of him.

His attackers silently left the way they had come.

Rex, ignoring Jon's anger said flatly, "We better sew that up," as he headed toward the medical room yet again.

Jon's anger slipped from him as he admitted defeat and followed Rex to have his arm taken care of, doubting he would ever be ready to seek his revenge.

Jon gritting his teeth through the pain of having another wound sewn up was shocked when Rex said, "You are ready."

"What are you talking about? You call that being ready?"

Rex stopped sewing and glanced at Jon, replying honestly. "Yes. You're ready. You handled yourself well and getting cut taught you things I couldn't teach you. You'll forever be aware of the possibility of a weapon being drawn on you."

Jon had come to respect the ugly little man, but knew he could not tell him, but he could say, "Thanks."

The hair stood up on Jon's neck as a shiver of warning washed over him. They were in danger. Suddenly, Agamemnon stepped into the room demanding, "What happened?"

Jon replied, "I was stupid."

Rex went back to sewing Jon's arm, saying without looking at Agamemnon, "He's ready."

"When you are finished bring him up to the house." Turning, he left.

Jon watching him walk away was again surprised by the man. He wondered how he had become what he was, ruthless. Jon suspected he was a killer. Glancing down at his arm as Rex finished with the last stitch he asked, thinking aloud. "How long have you known him?"

Rex paused as if considering answering Jon's question but instead stood up saying, "He's waiting."

Jon walked with Rex toward the mansion to find the same SUV limo waiting which had brought him here a month ago. Jon walked to the vehicle as the chauffeur opened the rear door, he stooped down to peer inside to discover a medium sized suitcase sitting on the rear seat. He jumped nervously, standing back up, when he suddenly heard Agamemnon say, as he extended a folder toward Jon, "Here is all the information I could gather. How can I reach you if I discover anything else?"

Jon had an uneasy feeling Agamemnon already knew how to contact him and said, "Text me."

Agamemnon threw back his head and laughed. "I recall now why you were the Captain. I'll text you." Then those inky black eyes stared with shocking intensity at Jon. "Happy hunting." And he turned and walked back into the mansion.

Jon stood for a few moments, again wondering what he had gotten himself into, but the rage burning in his gut pushed any sensible options from his mind. Someone must pay!

When they were on their way, he flipped open the folder, reading the names as he gazed at the photos of those involved in the initial kidnapping. Three men. Losers who had several run-ins with the law but nothing serious. Their last known addresses were included. Shouldn't be hard to eliminate them but he was after the big fish. He flipped through several more pages and finally found the name he was searching for, Nimrod. To his shocked disbelief he discovered that not only was Nimrod the man who had murdered Reggie, he had also been Nicole's pimp. Jon's heart thumped against his ribcage as he struggled to catch his breath, his excitement and need for revenge causing him to shake. He had not planned on seeking out the man in charge of Nicole's forced degradation, but it thrilled him to realize he was being given an awesome opportunity. He could kill two birds with one stone. He frantically searched for a photo of Nimrod and was disappointed when there wasn't one. He didn't need it anyway. He had complete confidence he would find him.

Next, he flipped open the suitcase and was thrilled to find a high-powered assault rifle with a scope, the likes of which Jon had never seen. He gently removed the scope from the suitcase and examined it, surprised at how advanced the technology had become. He really shouldn't be surprised, he thought, technology was advancing at mind blowing speed. He couldn't wait to use it. He closed the suitcase and leaned back resting his head on the headrest as his thoughts raced around in his mind.

CHAPTER 23

Within an hour he was being dropped off beside his parked jeep and speeding back to his penthouse. He decided to make the trip in one day and fifteen hours later he was home. He doubted anyone had yet discovered it was him who had taken Nicole, or killed the man sent to retrieve her, but he was about to find out. He parked the jeep in a general space and made his way toward the elevators, pleased to find a Security Guard he knew at the desk by the elevators who asked, "Mr. Sadler how can I help you?"

"I have been out of town a few weeks and was wondering if anyone left any messages."

The Security Guard searched the records on the computer and replied, "No, sir. No messages and no visitors, but I do need to inform you a man was shot and killed here about 6-8 weeks ago and the police did a thorough investigation. There hasn't been any more trouble."

"Thank you! Did they tell you what was the cause of the shooting? "

"No. They determined it must have been a robbery attempt and they haven't found the shooter yet."

"The world has become dangerous since the disappearance of all those people. Are they still rioting in Seattle?"

"Yes sir. Not as bad as at first but it seems every night something terrible happens."

"Thanks again, I've been on the East Coast the last few weeks exploring our options for expanding the business, so thanks for keeping me updated. If you hear anything else, please keep me informed. See you later."

"Anytime, Mr. Sadler and have a good day."

Jon feeling comfortable he hadn't been found out yet, made his way to his private elevator and was glad to step into his home. All appeared well. He did a quick check over the whole place including closets and the pantry and scanned the entire place for electronic devices. Satisfied all was safe he paused by the living room windows and gazed at the city. He realized he liked the city more than he wanted to admit to himself. He was glad to be home and looking out over the familiar skyline. Elliot Bay shimmered like a sheet of glass, not a ripple in sight, while the city below bustled with activity. No repairs had been made to the destroyed Ferris wheel. The gondola seats which had been throw all over the wharf appeared to have been removed but the piles of burned cars and debris remained.

He watched the sun set, casting golden rays across the still water, and decided tomorrow he would pay a little visit to the company office. He made his way to his home office to update himself on what was going on with the company, and to his shock and dismay he realized a coup was in the works for a takeover. He would put a stop to this tomorrow!

The next morning, he was up with the sunrise, anxious excitement coursing through his veins at the prospect of confronting those pushing for a takeover of Prism Technologies since his father couldn't be located. He looked forward to upsetting their plans.

As he took the elevator down to the parking garage, he changed his mind and stopped it at the first floor deciding he would walk to work and check out the city. Walking toward the office he noticed people lounging in the doorways and alleys eyeing him suspiciously. Quickening his step he realized it had not been a wise decision to walk as there was an air of barely contained hostility simmering beneath the surface of feigned laziness. He was relieved when he made it safely to the office.

Marching past his secretary he was surprised when she sputtered in shocked dismay. "Mr. Sadler sir, umm...where are you going, sir?"

He stopped and gazed at her with hard cold eyes. "You question me?"

She started to wring her hands nervously. "I'm sorry, sir, but...ummm...Mr. Ackman is using your office for a meeting."

"Good. I'm just in time."

And before the secretary could alert those in the meeting of his arrival, he burst through the door. "Good day, gentlemen and lady," acknowledging the secretary taking the minutes of the meeting. "I hope I haven't missed much," he declared.

Walking toward Mr. Ackman, stopping beside the chair he was sitting in at the head of the conference table, Jon glared at him silently, until Mr. Ackman's face flushed red with embarrassment and anger. He relinquished the seat moving to an empty chair further down the table as Jon took the recently vacated seat, smiling a deadly, condemning smile at the group staring at him in shock.

"I'm waiting to be informed of what this meeting is about," he demanded.

The group, as a whole, swung guilty glances at Mr. Ackman who suddenly looked like he was going to be sick. He swallowed nervously, causing his Adam's apple to bob up and down in his throat as he tried to regain his composure and stability.

He croaked, "We were discussing the absence of your father." He paused, swallowing again. "And what we needed to do to keep the company running."

Jon's icy eyes bore into Mr. Ackman. "Did this include confiscating my office for your use?"

Jon gazed around the table at those involved with the attempted take-over of the company, pausing to peer intently at each individual until they started to squirm. When he was satisfied everyone was suitably uncomfortable with his presence, he continued the meeting.

"My family has decided to take a leave of absence after the loss of my brother, and my father will return after his time of grieving. The person who takes it upon themselves to attempt a take-over of this company will be fired."

Jon glared at Mr. Ackman. "Mr. Ackman, you are hereby relieved of your position here at Prism Technologies. You have forfeited any severance pay, you will pack your belongings and vacate the premises immediately. You are forbidden from all Prism Technologies properties forever. Good day and good-bye." Mr. Ackman stood up on shaky legs glaring at Jon with intense anger and quietly left the room.

Jon said, "The rest of you are on two weeks suspension. You all are to leave now. I will have a meeting with each of you before you will be allowed to return to work."

He silently watched as they left the room and then stood up to survey his office. His personal belongings had been removed, so he called his secretary, "Ms. D'Orso!"

She hurried into his office, stopping in the door entrance visibly shaking. He didn't want to upset her this way, she had done nothing wrong, so he spoke softly and calmly trying to ease her discomfort. "Ms. D'Orso, I hope you can help me."

"Yes, sir, Mr. Sadler, how can I help?" she asked softly.

He smiled and was pleased when her shaking stopped. "Do you know where my belongings are?"

She smiled. "Yes, I do. When Mr. Ackman told me to dispose of them, I just couldn't bring myself to do that, instead I hid everything in my desk. I'll go get it for you."

"I knew I could count on you! Yes, please bring everything in here."

She rushed from his office and was back in minutes, her arms full of his awards, photos and other odds and ends he had collected over the years.

She rushed up to him smiling brightly, saying, "Here we go. Where do you want it?"

"Just put it on the conference table and I'll take care of it. And thank you, Ms. D'Orso."

After gently placing the objects on the table she turned, saying sincerely. "I'm so glad you are back. And I'm so sorry for your family's loss."

"Thank you," he answered, feeling guilty he had never taken the time to get to know her. She was a very kind and caring person. "That will be all for now."

She returned to her desk and Jon sat down in front of the computer to search his list of employees. He was quickly losing hope that he had an employee whom he could put in the position of his assistant when a name caught his attention. Thomas Getty. Jon read through the list of Thomas' education and his resume. He was impressed. Now to meet this man, who had such impressive job skills and had not been involved with the rest of management's deceit. He pushed the intercom button and told Ms. D'Orso to find Thomas Getty and send him in.

A few minutes later there was a knock on the door and Jon bid them enter. He stood up as Ms. D'Orso led a tall thin African American man into the room, who looked to be about 25 years old. He was impeccably dressed in a three-piece suit and confidently walked up to Jon's desk reaching forth his hand which Jon shook, glad to feel the strong grasp.

"Have a seat," Jon said pointing to a chair in front of his desk. "I have a few questions for you." Jon was glad to see only curiosity spark in his gaze. He was not intimidated by the boss.

"Mr. Sadler sir, I'llll do my best to answer any questions you have," he replied with confidence.

"I would like for you to tell me why you didn't get involved with Mr. Ackman's plans?"

Surprised by the question, Thomas answered, "I will not be a part of any dishonest actions." He paused gazing intently at Jon. Pleasing Jon with his inquisitive albeit cautious perusal of him. Thomas was wondering if he could trust Jon, and Jon admired a man that it mattered not whom he was confronting, he would make up his own mind, not being influenced by power or prestige. Thomas continued. "I didn't agree with Mr. Ackman's actions," he stated with conviction.

Jon said, "I don't know if you've heard my younger brother was murdered about two months ago and my parents have taken a leave of absence to grieve their loss."

"I offer my condolences, Mr. Sadler."

"The reason Mr. Ackman decided to take matters into his own hands was the absence of my father. I'll be busy with family affairs and need a man that I can trust and rely on to run the business when I'm away."

Thomas silently gazed at Jon not quite believing what he thought the boss was insinuating.

"Are you that man, Thomas Getty?"

Jon knew he had his man when disbelief flitted across his face, but Thomas recovered quickly, standing he offered his right hand to Jon. "Mr. Sadler, I'm most definitely your man."

Jon stood and shook his hand saying. "Then I'm pleased to offer you the position of Assistant CEO. You will run the business according to my directions and in the event you can't reach me you will have full authority to act as you decide, except you'll not have authority to sell any part of the company, its shares or stocks or its holdings. You will have the office next to mine and Ms. D'Orso will also be your secretary. You will receive a pay raise in accordance with your promotion. Tomorrow I'll have the legal paperwork ready to go over with you and I'll personally be in charge of your orientation for the next week at which time I'll do an evaluation."

Jon enjoyed watching the emotions cross Thomas' face and was pleased when he controlled his excitement to say. "I would be honored to accept your offer and I give you my word you'll not be disappointed."

"Great. I'll see you in the morning at 8 a.m. sharp."

"Yes sir, Mr. Sadler." And being unable to completely restrain his excitement he grabbed Jon's hand with both his hands and shook it briskly. "Thank you, Mr. Sadler!"

"See you tomorrow," Jon declared, dismissing Thomas. He had work to do. Thomas turned and rushed from the room wishing he had someone with whom to share his amazing news.

Jon called Ms. D'Orso into his office saying, "Ms. D'Orso, I'm making Thomas Getty my personal assistant and he'll run the company when I'm not available." Pleased to see her happiness at his news, he continued, "You'll also be his secretary, and I want you to take care of him like you have always taken care of me." And he winked at her. She blushed as unshed tears sparkled in her eyes.

"I'll start his orientation at eight tomorrow morning," Jon continued, "and I need you to make a packet of company information for him." He smiled at her. "I think you know as much as I do about the company, so I'll leave getting the information together in your capable hands."

"Thank you, Mr. Sadler. I'll have an orientation package ready in the morning." She smiled brightly up at him. "If I may be so bold as to say, I think Mr. Getty is an excellent choice."

Jon chuckled. "With such an exceptional endorsement, I'm pleased with my choice."

Ms. D'Orso was blushing again when she left the room with a decidedly perky step which made Jon happy. He sat back down at his computer to research exactly what had been planned. He discovered that Mr. Ackman was part of a much larger entity striving desperately to gain control of his father's company. The United States Government! They had come uncomfortably close to achieving their goal, and the more Jon read, he quickly came to realize he had only given himself a brief reprieve from the inevitable. As soon as the government recovered from his interference, his family would lose complete control of the company. He needed to get busy protecting what he could. He spent the rest of the day putting his plans in action. Realizing the sun was setting, he sent Ms. D'Orso home, called for the limo and was quickly back at his penthouse.

CHAPTER 24

After a quick dinner he sat down in front of his computer aching to research more on Reggie's killers. Jon admitted to himself it would have to wait until he finished his work with Prism Technologies. He needed to give his undivided attention to both problems and knew he couldn't do this if he was trying to do both at the same time, so he shut off the computer and stood up to go gaze at the now dark city below him. He wondered about Nicole and his family. How was she doing? He hoped she could recover from her trauma, knowing his mother was the best medicine for the girl because she could heal any broken heart. This was the reason he had to stay away from his family until he completed his revenge, he didn't want to hurt his mother by refusing her comfort.

After another night of troubled sleep interrupted by the ever-present nightmares, he crawled out of bed to get ready for another busy day. Today he drove the jeep to the office, getting a kick out of the security guard's reaction when he watched Jon exit the jeep.

"I took the Ferrari off the road. Too dangerous to drive it, someone might kill me for it. So, I'm driving this jeep for a while."

The guard smiled. "Smart idea, Mr. Sadler."

Jon was relieved the guard believed his excuse. Truth was that little red car was like a beacon drawing attention to himself and attention he didn't need.

He was surprised to find Ms. D'Orso already there and said as much to her. She replied, "I wanted to make sure the orientation folder was ready, and on your desk, before you arrived."

"Thank you Ms. D'Orso," he said as he entered his office. Picking up the folder, he sat down to leaf through the pages and found that Ms. D'Orso had been very thorough. He turned on the computer and did some research on Thomas Getty. He discovered Thomas had been adopted by a loving family when he was five years old and had had a very ordinary childhood, then to his dismay he read that his parents had been killed in a tragic car accident when he was 23. He could not find any record of there being siblings. He was an only child, without any records of him ever being married. He seemed to be alone in the world. Jon decided to make it his mission to find out who Mr. Thomas Getty was.

At 7:45 a.m. Ms. D'Orso announced Thomas Getty. Jon bid him enter and motioned him toward the conference table and they began the orientation, Jon learned quickly he had made an excellent choice. The man was intelligent and motivated, but most importantly he was honest.

The morning passed quickly, and Jon ordered lunch and while they ate, he questioned Thomas. "So, Thomas, I have been doing a little research about you and was wondering a few things."

Thomas was immediately on guard, he answered cautiously, "Yes sir, Mr. Sadler." He would only tell him what he felt was appropriate.

"I found out you were adopted and are an only child."

"Yes," Thomas said warily.

"You had wonderful parents."

This comment brought a slight smile to Thomas' lips. "Yes, they were. The best."

"I didn't find any records that you are married."

"No, sir. I've never been married."

"I haven't either. Maybe one day we'll each find the right woman."

Thomas smiled. "I hope so."

After lunch they continued the orientation. When the day was done, Jon told him they would continue tomorrow at the same time. Leaving the parking garage Jon decided that he would drive through the neighborhoods of the men he was searching for, he just couldn't sit still and do nothing. He was quickly in the suburban neighborhood and slowly driving by the small cookie cutter ranch house where one kidnapper lived. The neighborhood at one time had been a perfect oasis of modern middle-class America but now was run down with garbage piling up in front of some homes. Cars had been vandalized with windows broken and tires flattened. A pack of mangy dogs ran past his car stopping briefly to fight over the garbage, while a few teenagers halted their basketball game, glaring at him suspiciously and Jon realized he needed to head home before darkness settled completely.

He drove home without stopping, itching to take the rifle Agamemnon had given him and go execute the kidnapper now, but he knew lashing out in anger could cost him his own life. He would make a few more trips into the neighborhood searching for information on the man's habits.

The next four days were spent orienting Thomas, and Jon was thrilled when Saturday was finally here. Early Saturday morning he dressed in his worn out jeans, a faded denim shirt, slipped a baseball cap on his head, strapped his Glock under his arm and sat off walking to the parking garage where he had parked the beat up sedan he had left there after kidnapping Nicole and was shocked to find it parked exactly where he had left it with the keys still in the ignition. He climbed inside and drove toward the neighborhood he had already visited, thrilled when he drove past the house and found the man, he was searching for, sitting on the front steps. No one in the neighborhood paid any attention to Jon, he was just an ordinary guy driving a beat-up car.

Jon slowed the car as he drew near the house and rolling down the car window, he asked the kidnapper, "Hey, can I ask you something?"

The man eyed him suspiciously. "Yeah, I guess."

"Great. Do you know where Gene Hawks lives. I know it's on this road. I thought the house number was 1360 but I can't find it."

"Man, the house numbers don't go that high on this road and I don't know no nobody named Gene."

"Well, how about Orlando Jones?"

Jon was pleased to see the fear spark in the man's eyes, as he jumped to his feet waving his arms above his head yelling, "Hey, I don't know you!" as Jon took careful aim with his pistol pointed at the man's chest.

Jon whispered with intense, burning hatred, "You remember the boy you kidnapped and sold?"

"That wasn't my idea!"

"To bad." Jon pulled the trigger and sped away as the man fell backward onto the porch steps. Jon was feeling a glimmer of elation flicker through him at beginning his revenge, surprised his hands were shaking. His pistol was equipped with a silencer, so no one came to the dying man's aid. One down, two to go thought Jon, then he could take care of Nimrod.

Jon continued to the apartment complex where the other two men lived, driving around several run-down buildings searching for their addresses and was disappointed to discover they lived on opposite ends of the same complex. This was going to be more difficult. He realized he was not going to be so lucky this time, the neighborhood was very busy with teens playing basketball and adults lounging outside catching up on gossip or exchanging drugs. He needed to decide on a plan to get the men away from here or he would never be able to kill them. He had complete confidence he would come up with a plan as he drove back to the parking garage where the car had been parked and left it there again making sure he took the keys with him this time.

The following week he finished Thomas' orientation and feeling satisfied he could leave him in charge he said, "Thomas, I feel you're ready. How do you feel?"

Thomas answered confidently, "Yes sir, Mr. Sadler, I'm ready."

"Excellent! I have business to attend to and I may be gone for a couple weeks. You'll begin as my assistant on Monday." Handing him a slip of paper he continued, "Here is my cell phone number. Text me if you need me."

"You can depend on me, Mr. Sadler."

"Now we'll go to the company meeting in the main auditorium and I'll introduce you to the employees."

Thomas walked silently with Jon, still amazed at the turn of events in his life. He had never dreamt it would all happen so fast, and he would prove to Jon he had made the best choice possible. The company would be safe under his care. He strode out in front of the employees waiting expectantly and nodded when Jon introduced him. Then it was his turn to speak, short and sweet he decided. "Hello, I'm honored to be helping Mr. Sadler. We will make Mr. Amos Sadler proud of our job performance while he is away."

The employees clapped and Jon was pleased with his performance. Yes, an excellent choice indeed. He made his way back to his office leaving Thomas to mingle with the department heads. He did a double check making sure sensitive information about the company's financial status was secure from prying eyes. He didn't want Thomas to have access at this time.

An hour later Thomas entered his own office and Jon turned off his computer, locked his office door and knocked on Thomas' door. He entered when Thomas bid him.

"So how did the meeting go?" Jon asked.

"Very well, sir. I give you my word again, I'll run the company according to your direction." Thomas replied with the cool confidence of a man who was secure in his abilities.

"Text if you need me." And he left pausing by Ms. D'Orso's desk. She smiled up at him. He reached forth his hand toward her and dropped his office keys into her waiting palm. "I'll leave these with you."

"I'll lock them in my desk, Mr. Sadler. Have a safe trip."

"Thank you. See you in a couple of weeks."

He bent to whisper, causing her cheeks to flush a bright pink. "Take good care of Thomas."

She swallowed hard, stuttering a reply, "I...will...do...do my best."

"Thanks again," he said, and turning he marched down the hall to the elevator.

Jon drove to his penthouse without incident, quickly changed into his street clothes and in no time was cruising around the apartment complex. He stopped beside two men standing on the corner talking adamantly. They quieted when he rolled down the window. One reached his right hand toward his stomach and Jon realized he carried a handgun.

Jon asked, "Do you guys know Bull Dog?" He knew the man's real name was Vincent Franklin but knew he would get further using the man's nickname.

The taller of the two glared with intense distrust at Jon. "How do you know Bull Dog?"

"None of your business!" Jon spit out.

"Well, we don't know him."

"Fine, play your games. Tell him Reggie will meet him here tomorrow at 8 p.m." Jon pushed the gas pedal to the floor, spinning the wheels, leaving a cloud of burned rubber hovering over the two men.

The next evening as the sun was hanging low in the sky casting a pale orange glow over the landscape Jon saw four men waiting at the meeting spot. He stopped the car across the parking lot and rolling down the passenger side window said, "I want Bull Dog to come over here by himself. What we have to talk about is private."

A man stepped out from the group, taking a few steps and Jon yelled, "I don't know who that jerk is. Quit playing games or someone is going to die. I want Bull Dog!"

Finally, Bull Dog stepped forward signaling the others not to move saying, "I got this."

When he made his way to the car Bull Dog bent down to glance at Jon through the open window. "I don't know you!"

"No, but I know you." Jon answered pointing his 44-magnum with the silencer, at the man's head. "Get in," he demanded. "If you flinch at all, or try to alert your friends, I'll kill all of you and your little brother Travis," Jon threatened, knowing the threat to his brother would motivate him.

"Just so you know I'm serious, that's your little brother over there throwing hoops. The one wearing the navy shirt. Now get in, or I'll kill him now."

Jon was pleased to watch the man's eyes grow wide with fear as he slowly opened the door and was sliding into the car when the rest of his gang started to move. "I'm just going for a ride."

Once again Jon sped away, keeping his right hand on the pistol resting in his lap saying, "Put both hands on the dash where I can keep an eye on them."

Bull Dog placed his outstretched hands on the dash in front of him, asking nervously, "What have I done? I don't know you!"

Jon stopped the car a couple miles away, deep inside a neighborhood park. It was deserted because the sun had set, and darkness was descending.

Jon demanded, "Let's go for a walk and talk about Reggie."

Bull Dog glanced out into the dark park and started to shake, "NO!"

Jon pushed the silencer hard into Bull Dog's ribs, "Yes!" and was caught off guard with the flash of a knife blade. He hit the man's wrist hard with the gun but not before he was cut on his left forearm. He hated knives! Bull Dog yelled, "I think you broke my hand!" as Jon hissed coldly, "Get out!"

They both climbed out of the jeep, Jon motioning for Bull Dog to walk down the forest path. Jon followed, ignoring the blood slowly dripping from the fingers of his left hand.

Bull Dog said, "I don't know anybody named Reggie and I sure don't know you."

Bull Dog's blood ran cold when Jon chuckled with an evil he understood all too well. "Sure, you do. You know of a boy named Reggie. You know, the one you sold for two million dollars."

Bull Dog stumbled and fell hard to his knees. "That was Orlando's doing. I had nothing to do with it," he pleaded resting on his hands and knees.

"Nimrod murdered him and that makes you responsible."

"Who are you?" Bull Dog whined with fear.

"Reggie's big brother. You killed my little brother, but I won't kill yours."

Jon cocked the gun as Bull Dog pleaded, "No, wait! I'm tellin' the truth. It was Orlan...."

He never finished his sentence when Jon pulled the trigger aiming at his head. He shot him once more to make sure he was dead, then turned and walked away. Two down, one to go.

As Jon reached for the car door knob the blood which had run down his arm onto his hand caused his hand to slip. He glanced at his bloody hand and started to shake. What was he doing? He had just stood over a man and shot him in cold blood, but the man had helped murder Reggie. Hardening his heart, he slid into the driver's seat and headed home.

He made it back to his penthouse without incident, and cleaned the wound on his arm, glad it wasn't bad enough to need stitches. After a shower, he wrapped the wound with gauze, grabbed a bite to eat and went to sleep. Tomorrow he would go looking for the last kidnapper.

CHAPTER 25

The next day as Jon was searching the apartment complex, again looking for ways he could lure the last man away from his apartment, he felt his phone vibrate and looked to see who was calling him surprised to see Thomas' name quickly followed by Ms. D'Orso's name. Both of them were trying to reach him! Something was happening! He dialed Thomas who answered promptly, "Mr. Sadler?"

"Yes, Thomas. What's going on?"

"Men are at Ms. D'Orso's desk claiming to be from the FBI saying they are here to arrest you for fraud. I made sure your office door is locked and I have locked myself in my office."

Jon was surprised they were acting so quickly. He wondered what the government wanted with his father's company, but right now he needed to concentrate on helping Thomas and his secretary.

"Calm down, Thomas. Go to them and tell them what you know."

"But, Mr. Sadler, I don't know anything!"

"Exactly! Don't worry about me. I'll call you back later. Just cooperate with them. I don't want you getting arrested."

"Yes, sir," Thomas replied, sighing when the phone went dead.

What was happening in the world? He knew the Sadler's were honest. Who could be accusing them of fraud? Taking a deep breath to steady his nerves, he left his office and confronted the two men talking to Ms. D'Orso.

"Hello, gentlemen, how may I be of assistance?" Thomas asked.

As he drew closer to the men, he noticed two police officers blocking the entrance to the offices.

"Are you Mr. Jonathan Sadler?" one asked.

"No, sir. Mr. Sadler and his family are away at this time, I'm Thomas Getty, Assistant CEO. How can I help you?"

"Where can we reach them?"

"I'm sorry but they recently suffered the loss of their son and are in mourning and I don't know where they are."

One of the police officers spoke. "He is telling the truth. Their son was brutally murdered a couple months ago."

The man doing the questioning asked, "Well, I'm sure you have a way to contact him?"

"He contacts me," Thomas replied evasively.

The man's eyes narrowed as he glared at Thomas. "Tell me how to contact him or I will have you arrested."

Thomas noticed Ms. D'Orso start to cry and felt distress that he was going to add to her anguish. "Lock up the office, Ms. D'Orso, as it appears I'll be occupied elsewhere."

"But Mr. Getty!" she pleaded.

He interrupted her. "Gentlemen, may I please use the intercom to announce to the employees what is transpiring?"

"No! We'll manage. Arrest him," he instructed the police officer.

After they had cuffed his hands behind his back Thomas calmly let them lead him past Ms. D'Orso and he winked at her saying, "I know you'll handle securing the office."

He was pleased to see she caught his drift when she smiled, and replied, "Yes sir. You can depend on me."

One of the police officers shoved him in the back. "Shut up and get moving."

Thomas turned away from Ms. D'Orso and walked toward the elevator wondering fearfully what might be in store for him.

Ms. D'Orso waited until they all left and rushed into Jon's and Thomas' offices, grabbing Jon's laptop and Thomas' phone which he had left on his desk top. She glanced around trying to remember what else might hold contact information and confident she had everything she hid the items in her purse deciding it was the safest place to hide them. Quickly she relocked Jon's office and was in the process of shutting her computer down when the strange men reentered her office accompanied by Mr. Ackman. They marched past her desk and tried to open Jon's office door.

The one which seemed to be in charge barked at her to open the door causing her to start shaking as she rushed to unlock the door.

When they entered the office, Mr. Ackman demanded vehemently, "You can leave now. We know longer need your help."

"But Mr. Getty told me...." She didn't finish as he said menacingly, "Take your belongings and leave. You are terminated as of now. Do not return to this building."

She left the office, tears streaming down her cheeks as she gathered her personal belongings and quietly left the building.

She went straight home and sent a text message to Jon, "Mr. Sadler, they have arrested Mr. Getty, and Mr. Ackman fired me." She had started to type she had his laptop and Thomas' phone but suddenly thought they might be monitoring her, so she deleted that information from the text.

Her phone rang within minutes. It was Jon. "Ms. D'Orso, I'm so sorry this has happened. Don't worry about Thomas, I'll take care of him. Are you ok?"

"Yes, sir, just upset."

"I understand. Do you feel safe at your home?"

"Yes, sir."

"I'm here if you need me." He hung up.

Thomas sat in the holding cell becoming more worried with each passing hour. What was going to happen to him? He wasn't sure he was enjoying this roller coaster ride he was on. One day the assistant to the CEO, the next day arrested, and fired. He leaned forward with his elbows on his knees, as he ran his hands through his hair. He was in trouble! Suddenly the main door swung open, and a police officer entered, followed by a man Thomas had never seen. They walked up to his cell and the officer opened the door saying, "You're free to go."

Thomas stood up gazing at the men with confusion. The stranger spoke. "I'm Mr. Wingate, your lawyer."

"My lawyer?" Thomas asked in disbelief.

"Yes. Come with me and we'll talk on the way to your home."

The lawyer led him from the building and Thomas was surprised to see a black limo waiting. The chauffer quickly opened the door as the lawyer led him to the waiting car. Thomas, bending down to climb into the limo was shocked to see Jon waiting inside signaling for him to remain quiet.

Once Thomas and the lawyer were seated in the limo and they were moving Jon said, "Thomas, I'm so sorry this has happened. I knew the government was planning to take control of the company, I just didn't think it would happen this fast." Thomas started to interrupt but Jon stopped him and continued, "Do not worry about going to jail, Mr. Wingate is going to negotiate with everyone involved and reassure the government my family is capitulating to their demands."

This time Thomas was successful, interrupting. "But, Mr. Sadler. It's yours. Fight for it!"

"No, Thomas. I can't win. I don't completely understand why they want my father's company, but it must have something to do with our computer programming abilities."

They dropped Mr. Wingate at his office and continued to Thomas' small home, Jon asking, "Can I come inside and talk with you privately, Thomas?"

"Sure."

Once they were seated in the living room Jon said, "Thomas, I know you have no family. I'm wondering what you will do now?"

Thomas glanced at this man who had given him an opportunity beyond his wildest dreams, wondering what he was up to now. He replied, "Take care of myself like I always have."

"I have a proposition for you," Jon said.

Thomas wasn't sure he wanted to even hear what Jon had to say this time, he replied, "I think I'll be fine."

Jon continued, ignoring Thomas. "I think things are going to get very bad and you will not be safe."

"What are you talking about?" said Thomas. Looking dismayed.

"Well, I believe that the apocalypse all those preppers have been talking about is upon us."

Thomas' curiosity was piqued. "Really?"

"Really. I think the world is going to become a very dangerous place and I think we both need to go into hiding until we see what is going to happen with the government takeover of my company."

"Hide where?"

"I have a place. Are you interested?"

"Sure. Why not?" As insecure as he was with Jon, the government and the threat of jail terrified him.

"Pack what you want to take with you. I'll be waiting in the limo."

"Now?"

"Yes. Now."

Thomas smiled off-handedly. "If you say so, boss. I sure don't want to visit that jail again."

Jon chuckled as he rose to go wait in the limo.

Once Thomas was in the limo, Jon directed the driver to take them back to the office building. Thomas broke out in a cold sweat. "What are you doing, Mr. Sadler?"

"Just getting my Jeep. It's less conspicuous than this limo. We'll be careful."

They retrieved the jeep without difficulty and the next stop was another small house. Surely this was not Jon's home, thought Thomas, maybe the hideout. "Come with me, Thomas."

They left the jeep together and Jon knocked on the door of the house. Ms. D'Orso cautiously peeked through the narrow gap made when she barely opened the door. "Mr. Sadler sir. Why are you here? I'm so glad to see you! Come in." She swung the door open wide and both men entered the modest home.

"I needed to make sure you are alright," Jon said. "And I couldn't talk to you on the phone."

"Would you like something to drink?" she asked.

Thomas declared, "Yes, I would!"

"Tea or coffee?"

"Tea."

Jon said, "Bring us both a glass of tea. Please."

"Yes sir, Mr. Sadler."

Jon grabbed her hand and said with heartfelt regret, "I know I was not a very good boss and for that I'm sorry. I would be honored if you would consider me a friend and call me Jon."

She blushed, "Yes sir, Mr. Sadler...umm...I mean Jon. I'll be right back with the tea."

She quickly returned carrying two glasses of tea and her large purse, causing Jon to wonder why a woman needed something as big as a small suitcase. After she handed each man his glass she sat down across from Jon and opening her purse, handed him the laptop and Thomas his phone.

Jon smiled. "You are a gem! Thank you, Ms. D'Orso!"

"If I'm to call you Jon then you must call me Emily," she replied.

"Ok. Emily. Now I have a question for you. Will you be, ok?"

"Yes. I'm going to stay with my son and his wife in Mountlake Terrace for a while, Seattle is not safe. He should be here to pick me up in about an hour."

"Great!" Jon declared. "You know how to reach me if you need me. Take care."

"I will. You be careful, Jon."

And they left her alone, both men hoping she would be ok. As they drove away Jon told Thomas, "I have a cabin in the mountains that we can hide at until we are sure we'll be safe. It'll take about an hour to get there. Are you hungry? We can grab a quick bite to eat."

"Sure. Any place will be fine."

Jon, not wanting to waste time drove through the drive thru of a local hamburger joint and ordered their meals to go and they ate on the road. Neither man said much, both lost in their own thoughts and soon Jon was pushing the button again to open the gate to his cabin, missing Nicole's joyful interest in the surroundings.

Thomas gazed around in silence, finally speaking when the cabin came into view. "So, this is your place?"

"One of many, but it's my favorite place."

Jon parked the jeep and showed Thomas the cabin and the same room he had shown Nicole just a couple months ago, saying, "This will be your room while we are here."

"How long will we stay here?"

"Hopefully not long. I have something I have to finish."

Jon still managed to set Thomas on edge. He wasn't sure he could completely trust the man. Thomas sensed he wasn't telling him everything and he wished he could just walk away. He wished he had never accepted Jon's offer to be his assistant, wished he had never heard of Prism Technologies, then he wouldn't be hiding like a common criminal when he had done no wrong, depending on this man who had turned his life upside down. It rankled him that he had to depend on Jon, but he saw no other option at the moment.

Thomas needed to be alone to think. "I'm tired. I think I'll go to bed."

'I'm tired myself. See ya in the morning."

CHAPTER 26

The next couple of days they discussed Jon's plans for his company. On the morning of the third day, they were awakened by a sound they had never heard before. They met each other in the hall as the earth swayed under their feet.

"Earthquake?" Thomas asked.

"I don't think so," Jon said in disbelief. "I think it might have been a bomb."

Jon turned on the TV and they watched in shocked horror as the news anchor said, "It has been confirmed that a nuclear device has been detonated in Seattle. We are waiting for the Governor of Washington to speak at a press conference shortly."

"A nuclear bomb?" Thomas whispered.

Jon silently watched the TV, trying very hard not to have a flashback to his time in Iraq, his heart pounding as he struggled to catch his breath. Thomas shook him by his arm. "Jon, you ok?"

Jon focused on him, which helped to calm him. "Yeah, I'm ok, just shocked."

"Do you think much is left? I wonder about the employees. Ms. D'Orso. I hope she made it to Mountlake Terrace."

"So do I, Thomas," he replied grabbing his phone and to his dismay realized the phone towers must be damaged because the phone screen read 'No service available'. "We can't call her, service is out."

Over the next hour they watched in silence as the Governor talked but didn't say much, a military officer talked but didn't say much and the police did the same. Seemed no one knew anything. Jon searched his laptop, finally finding several private videos and drone videos of the destruction and was appalled. It appeared most of downtown Seattle had been leveled, including his penthouse and the Prism Technologies office building, many of the suburbs were piles of rubble with much of it on fire, the airport was destroyed, and the Space Needle had been disintegrated.

While searching Jon discovered a video made by a man about his age who intrigued him. He remembered Reggie mentioning the Rapture and this stranger was talking about the Rapture and was making statements about what was going to happen in the world. He claimed that this nuclear bomb was just the beginning. He said God was going to begin raining down judgments on the world. If what he said was true, the world was in trouble.

Jon realized with deep disappointment he probably would never find the third man involved with his brother's kidnapping and decided he must concentrate on Nimrod. He also had to get to the bunker and check on his family. He decided it was too dangerous to call so he would have to make a trip to Virginia.

He asked Thomas, "My business was in Seattle so I will not be able to finish it for now, and I have another proposition for you. My family has a secure bunker in which they are presently hiding, would you be interested in going there for your safety?"

Thomas gazed at him in stunned silence. Bunker? His world just got crazier. "A bunker, what are you talking about?"

"One of those underground living spaces that'll keep us safe from the insanity in the world at the moment and even protect us from nuclear bombs."

"You want me to live underground? I don't think so." Thomas desperately wanted his world to stop spinning.

Jon asked with concern. "Where will you go, Thomas?"

Thomas jumped up and started to pace. He hoped he would wake up and the nightmare would end, but he knew that wasn't possible, and Jon made a valid point. Where could he go? His house was gone, his job was gone, and he didn't know if the US government might be looking for him. Suddenly the bunker option seemed like a good idea. Hiding seemed like an excellent idea!

He glanced at the man who had turned his world upside down and reluctantly said, "You make a strong case, Jon. I guess the wisest choice is to go with you. Where will we be going?"

"Virginia." Jon was trying very hard to maintain his composure and not laugh, but the constant waves of emotions playing out on Thomas' face was very entertaining.

"VIRGINIA!" Thomas threw his arms up. "Forget it, just forget it! I change my mind. I'm not going anywhere!"

Jon sat silently watching the frustrated, frightened young man pace and when he paused to look at him, Jon continued, "My father grew up in western Virginia and knows the mountains very well. He wanted to go there to hide and be safe when an apocalypse happened. I admit, at first, I thought he was crazy. He bought an abandoned bunker and had it refurbished and made safe for living. It is difficult for me to admit he was right, but he was right. So now I'm going to check on them and you are welcome to come along and live there if you want. It's up to you Thomas. I know the world has gone crazy and insane, but I'm telling you the truth."

Thomas asked softly, "Can't I just stay here?"

"Sure, you can, but you need to keep in mind those men who took over my business know about this cabin too."

Thomas plopped down in a chair, angry with himself for feeling so helpless. He knew he had no decent alternative. "I'll go with you, but how'll we get there?"

"I hope we can fly out of Spokane, but if not, we'll have to drive."

"When will we leave?"

"After lunch."

"I'll be ready," Thomas said despondently.

They drove the jeep into Spokane without any problems and when Jon pulled into a discount store parking lot Thomas gazed at him suspiciously. "What're we doing now?"

"I got to grab a couple of things. If you need anything get it now," Jon replied heading into the store to buy several cheap cell phones as his supply was running low.

Both men returned to the jeep at about the same time, Jon saying, "You need to throw away your cell phone because they can track us." He handed Thomas another phone. "Use this one until the minutes run out, then throw it away and I'll give you another one when you need it."

"Do you think this is really necessary?" Thomas asked with skepticism.

"Yes, I do. Those men who claimed to be FBI were really from the deep state of the United States Government. They may track us using our phones, so we need to get rid of them."

Thomas sighed, handed his phone to Jon and took the new one he gave him. Jon placed the phone on the asphalt and stomped on it shattering it into pieces. Thomas said again, "Is that necessary?"

Jon glanced at Thomas with a hint of frustrated disbelief as he picked up most of the phone pieces, tossing them in a trash can. "I thought you knew something about Prism Technologies and what we do and would understand how important it is that we do this."

Jon suddenly had a flash of revelation, the government knew about the company's internet tracking abilities, the top-secret ones, the ones Jon had thought were secure from prying eyes, he realized there had been a spy in the company. He knew the government would murder his family or lock his family away for the rest of their lives, if they could find them. He had to be even more careful than he had realized.

Thomas replied, "I do understand. I'm just frustrated and upset."

"You need to get yourself together, Thomas. I need you to be alert and watch who you talk to and what you say. I'll do my best to get us safely to the bunker." He gazed intently at Thomas, "Can I still depend on you?"

"Yes, Jon. I give you my word."

Jon was thrilled to see airplanes landing at the airport, but discovered the airport was a circus, with everyone who couldn't fly out of Seattle attempting to catch a flight at Spokane. After waiting in line for two hours Jon finally had tickets for them to fly to Roanoke the next evening. Next Jon managed to get two motel rooms by bribing the owner with an exorbitant amount of cash. No problem, at least they had someplace decent to rest for the night.

After he had settled in, Jon knocked on Thomas' door. "Come on, let's go get a good meal. My treat. I know you have got to be starving like me."

Thomas grinned, "You don't have to ask twice." he said pulling the door shut behind him.

After a filling meal at a local restaurant, they both slept well and woke up ready to go the next morning.

CHAPTER 27

Jon spent the few hours before checkout, searching for information on Nimrod. Agamemnon had given him just enough info to make his curiosity burn. The only thing he seemed to be able to discover was that Nimrod was an ancient Babylonian emperor who had tried to build a tower to get to heaven. Interesting story he thought to himself, but it was useless to him. He reluctantly admitted to himself the only chance he would have at finding the man would be to search the dark web for underage prostitutes. Breathing hard, with trepidation, he plunged into the unknown and after taking a quick glance he felt sick to his stomach. How could monsters like this exist? His worst nightmares could not imagine such evil. He searched the Seattle area trying to keep his eyes focused away from the horrifying photos and was shocked when a site titled Babylon popped up. He couldn't hardly believe his luck. A sudden knock interrupted him, and he quickly turned off the computer slamming it shut.

Thomas said through the closed door, "You ready to leave, Jon?"

"Coming," he called, stuffing the computer into his carryon bag. He grabbed the handle to his suitcase, and swinging the door open, they left the motel.

Once they were sitting in the jeep Thomas asked, "What do we do now? We have four hours before we can check in at the airport."

"I guess we can wait at the airport. I don't want to take any chances missing our flight," Jon replied.

They found an empty corner in the airport and started their wait. Jon never had time to just sit and waste time and he had to admit to himself watching the people coming and going was rather interesting. Time passed slowly and soon it was time to board the plane. They arrived in Roanoke at midnight, Jon rented a car, paid for a night's stay at the hotel he had stayed at several times before and told Thomas they would leave for the bunker at daybreak. Jon didn't have the stomach to do any research on Nimrod or watch TV, so he rested quietly until he dozed off and was awakened by a nightmare. Swinging his feet out of bed he went searching for his aspirin, swallowing a couple, he noticed the time was 5 a.m. and decided he would just stay up. At 6 a.m. he wandered toward the front lobby glad to see the front desk clerk putting out the donuts, honey buns, rainbow colored cereal and fruit that was supposed to be breakfast. Shaking his head in disbelief that people really ate this stuff, he grabbed a couple pieces of fruit and a cup of coffee, that was surprisingly good, and headed back to his room.

An hour later they were headed north on the Blue Ridge Parkway. After about a one-hour drive Jon parked the jeep in the parking lot of a small restaurant nestled in the trees at one of the entrances to the Appalachian Trail.

"Be back in a minute," Jon said as he headed inside. A minute later he was back and parked the car at the far side of the parking lot. "They gave me permission to park here for a couple of days." Jon signaled for Thomas to follow him. "Come on. You ready for a hike on the Trail?"

Thomas glared at him. "You're kidding, right?"

Jon replied nonchalantly. "No," he said innocently. "We're going for a hike." Jon just couldn't help himself. He didn't know why he got such delight out of teasing Thomas, but he did.

"You're crazy!"

"Oh, come on, it'll be good for you."

"Take me back to the airport!"

Jon relented. "Hey, it's ok. I'm just kiddin. We have to hike in. It's the only way to get there. It won't take long. Really."

Thomas glared angrily at Jon as he grabbed his suitcase and duffle bag and marched toward the trail. Jon followed him saying, "Follow me. I give you my word we'll go straight there. I won't lead you in circles."

Thomas still glaring at Jon refused to talk to him and followed silently. Jon gave up trying to engage him in a conversation and hiked briskly along the trail and eventually turned into the thick forest, leading Thomas to the meadow where he sometimes landed a helicopter.

He paused, casting a quick glance around the meadow saying, "We don't have far to go now. It's past that tree line." Jon pointed across the meadow and Thomas could see nothing but trees, "All I can say is something better be there besides trees."

Jon chuckled and set off across the meadow. When he slowed, Thomas noticed a steep rock face reaching for the blue sky. He was surprised when Jon walked around the rock face, realizing it was a huge boulder, and pushed through the thick growth of brush and trees to a hidden steel door. Jon pushed a code into the control panel and the door slid silently open. Thomas was surprised when they entered a small foyer with a tunnel extending into the interior. Thomas felt his heart jump in his chest with fear when a large man entered the tunnel pointing an AK-47 at them.

When the man entered the foyer, he propped the rifle against the wall declaring, "Jon! Wow what a surprise! So glad to see you!" and he slapped Jon on the back. The man paused, glancing at Thomas.

Jon said, "Clay, meet Thomas, my assistant from Prism Technologies. I'll update the family when we're all together."

They walked down the tunnel and Thomas was surprised when they entered the main area. Jon hadn't been kidding. His family was actually living in a bunker. Jon's family rushed him as someone yelled, "Hurry up Nicole, Jon is here!"

An older lady, two young women, and a disabled old man surrounded Jon, when suddenly someone squealed, "JON!" and Thomas watched the most beautiful young woman he had ever seen run up to Jon and throw her arms around his neck.

Jon laughed and twirled her around once then set her on her feet. "Are you here to stay?" she asked.

"No, Nicole." he pulled Thomas forward. "I came here to bring my friend Thomas to stay with us for a while, and I must leave tomorrow morning."

His family welcomed Thomas as Jon introduced him to them, then Jon grew serious. "I don't know if you have heard, but a nuclear bomb has gone off in Seattle. I'm not sure if any have exploded in any other cities. Dad our office, my penthouse and your home are gone. The whole downtown area has been flattened."

The women were crying. Jon continued. "Dad, Clay, can I talk to you in private?"

They agreed and followed Amos to the hall which led to his bedroom. Once inside the bedroom Amos turned toward Jon. "What's wrong, son?"

"Dad, the US government has taken control of your company. I stashed away what assets I could before they confiscated the company. I believe Mr. Ackman was a spy. He was part of the takeover and tried to have me arrested but arrested Thomas instead. I had to bring him here for his own safety. The world is going crazy!"

Amos gazed at Jon, stunned by the turn of events, and asked, "You were right, Jon, the apocalypse is here. Do they have any idea we are here?"

"No, Dad. We paid cash for everything so there is no trail for them to follow. I paid the construction crew well; they will keep our secret. I even made several inquiries about possible real estate purchases we could use to open an office in Roanoke to hide the reasons I was flying in and out of Roanoke."

Amos was impressed with his son. "Well done, Jon."

"I made Thomas my assistant and they had him arrested because he wouldn't tell them where I was, and when the bomb destroyed Seattle, I discovered he has no family and nowhere to go, so that is why I brought him here."

Jon said to Clay, "I believe he is a city boy, Clay. Kind of soft. Probably never even held a gun in his hand. See what you can do with him."

Clay chuckled. "Sure thing. Since you said you are leaving tomorrow, I take it you are still searching."

"Yes," Jon replied softly. "Still looking."

Amos suddenly felt a shiver of fear shudder through his body. "Jon, leave it alone. Stay here."

Jon glanced at his father, anger and anguish battling in his eyes. "I have to finish, Dad."

Amos had never pleaded with anyone for anything in his life. "Please, Jon. Your mother is so worried about you."

"Sorry, Dad, but I have to finish."

Amos demanded, "Listen to me! I'm telling you to stay here!"

Jon replied harshly, his blue eyes burning with an anger that frightened Amos. "No, Dad! You listen to me! I will finish what I have started!"

Amos hung his head, admitting defeat. "Be careful, Jon."

They went back to the living area and now it was Jon's turn to be surprised when Clay said seriously, "Jon, I have some news for you."

Jon watched silently as Katie walked up to Clay's side and he wrapped his arm around her shoulder pulling her close to him. "I hope you will be happy for us." He paused and Katie rushed on excitedly, "We got married, Jon!"

"Married? How?" Jon asked, very concerned. "Did you leave the bunker?"

Clay smiled reassuringly, "Fred has a brother who is a preacher and the two of us went over to Fred's place and got married. We were very careful. We didn't even get a marriage license. We made our promises to each other. It's real to us, Jon, and we feel God approves."

Jon glanced at his father. "You approved of this?"

"Yes, Jon."

Jon was surprised and then happy. He hugged Katie and slapped Clay on the back. "Couldn't ask for a better brother-in-law, and you better take care of her."

Next, Jon sat down beside his mother and talked quietly with her. He could feel her calmness settle on him bringing relief to his tortured soul. He needed her, he would never admit it to himself, but he needed her. She had always been the steady soothing ally which had helped him stand against the storms of his life, but he must protect her from the evil in this world, so he steered the conversation away from himself and talked with her about Nicole and about Katie's wedding. He was pleased to learn Nicole was settling in well and was recovering from her ordeal. Betty asked him about Thomas, and he explained the situation to her. She fluttered over to the nervous young man and spread her wings of comfort around him, as Jon stood up saying he was going for a ride to check on the property, Nicole asking to go along. He agreed and they left. Thomas watched them leave wondering what the story was about Nicole, she appeared too young to be Jon's wife, maybe someone's daughter. He had a strong feeling she wasn't Mr. and Mrs. Sadler's daughter. He looked forward to discovering who she was.

Jon and Nicole saddled the horses and rode cautiously out into the world. Nicole was thrilled he had let her come, and she had him all too herself.

She burst forth enthusiastically, "Jon, thank you so much for bringing me here! Your family has been so wonderful, and I feel like I'm part of the family. Your mom is the most amazing person I have ever met, and your sisters are great. I'm so happy for Katie and Clay! Who is that Thomas guy and where did he come from?" She didn't give him a chance to answer her comments, as she continued talking nonstop. He rode beside her in silence enjoying her youthful distraction. It was impossible to be depressed around her. They had almost finished the circuit of the meadow when abruptly she stopped talking and glanced at him.

He stopped his horse as she pulled her horse up beside his. "Anything wrong, Nicole?" he asked.

"No. I just realized I have been running my mouth too much. I'm sorry."

Jon reached over and patted her on her forearm. "You talk all you want to, sweetheart. I enjoy listening to you."

"Please don't leave us. We need you here," she pleaded.

Jon replied seriously. "Nicole, the world is getting very bad, very fast, and I have things I need to finish before I can stay here permanently."

"Please be careful," she relented, realizing she couldn't change his mind.

"I will," he said kicking the horse into motion. "Time to go back inside."

He enjoyed the evening with his family and friends, telling Clay in private he would be bringing in weapon supplies and would contact him when he needed help. Early the next morning he started his hike back to the rental car. He made his way quickly to the car and was back at Roanoke, where he paid for a couple nights' stay at a local hotel to search the computer for information on Nimrod, then he would know where he needed to fly. He had gone to Roanoke instead of staying with his family because he did not want to take a chance of his family accidently discovering his searches on the dark web or his where abouts being discovered by the US government. He discovered that Martial Law had been declared and the United Nations was going to be sending in troops to help control the rioting crowds in the big cities. So far only Seattle had been destroyed by the nuclear bomb.

CHAPTER 28

Over the next two days he never left the room, having his meals delivered to his room. He dove deep into the webpage Babylon and the deeper he went the darker his world became, an evil so intense he couldn't fight it, was settling on his soul, but he must find Nimrod no matter what it cost him. He must avenge Reggie's death. He owed that to Reggie and to their parents.

He discovered Nimrod's center of operation was in Las Vegas and was soon on an airplane heading there. It had been many years since he had visited there, and the place was still as loud and flashy as he remembered, with no indication of the turmoil the rest of the world was suffering. He grabbed his rental car and was quickly at the Bellagio, the fountains still dancing in time to the music as the lights flashed. He checked in and made his way to his room refusing the bellboy's help and ordered room service for dinner. After dinner he lay down intending to just take a nap and slept until daybreak without dreaming, waking refreshed. He couldn't remember when he had last slept without nightmares.

He dressed in jeans and a t-shirt and headed north on I-15 into the desert with the intention of finding the brothel he had learned about on the Babylon site. Just south of the NASCAR raceway he exited the interstate and started searching the suburban neighborhood thinking the families living here would be shocked if they knew what was happening right under their noses. He finally found the address he was looking for and slowed, glancing at the high wrought iron gates locking out the world and locking in the nightmare of what was going on behind those menacing gates. He noticed the security cameras and continued driving past the gates. How was he going to find the courage to enter this hell?

First, he needed to contact his private supplier to get the weapons he needed for himself because the nuclear attack had destroyed the guns and ammo he had stored at his penthouse and he realized he needed to go ahead and have the rest of the supplies he had ordered for the bunker delivered, so he could transport them before the government started to set up roadblocks across the country. Finding Nimrod would have to wait a couple more weeks. When he returned to the hotel, he parked the car and walked to the nearest moving van rental company and rented a small panel truck in which to transport the illegal weapons he had purchased. After paying for a two week stay at the Bellagio, he started his trip to the rendezvous with the gun runners, men like himself, who believed their 2nd Amendment rights were being destroyed and had created an underground network to purchase what they needed, away from the prying eyes of law enforcement.

In two days, he was at the desert pickup, a large steel Quonset hut storage building on the outskirts of El Paso. He had met the men several times to discuss what he needed and knew he could trust them. Everything went smoothly and he was soon on his way to the bunker. Stopping at a cheap motel he purchased a paper road map, spending a couple hours marking the route he was going to take, keeping to the back roads because he knew the interstates were becoming dangerous, after the bomb in Seattle, with increased military and law enforcement patrolling.

His travels were going fine until he crossed into Tennessee and was stopped at a check point. When his turn came to be questioned, he was ready with his driver's license but not ready for the attitude of the soldier who ordered him out of the truck saying harshly, "We need you to unlock the back of this truck."

Jon replied calmly not wanting to arouse suspicion. "You guys looking for somebody?"

"Just open the truck!" He pointed his rifle at Jon signaling him to move to the back of the truck.

Jon walked to the back, unlocked and opened the door revealing several boxes and furniture.

"What are you hauling?"

"Just moving closer to my family in Virginia. Lost some family in the disappearance and I'm moving to be with the ones I have left."

"Open the box!" demanded the one holding the rifle aimed at him, pointing to the box he wanted Jon to remove from the van.

"Why? It's just household goods and stuff."

The man took a threatening step toward Jon, and Jon reached up, and grabbed the box, exposing a dresser, and placed it at the man's feet. The man motioned for his partner to open the box, who quickly had it open and rummaged through the pots and pans inside.

Jon controlled his mounting anger and biting his tongue stood still as another box was removed and its contents strewn on the ground.

The one holding the rifle said, "Good grief! Put your junk back in the truck and get moving."

Jon, keeping his mouth shut, haphazardly repacked the boxes, shoving them back in the truck and slammed the door shut hissing, "Can I go now?"

The man's eyes narrowed menacingly. "Leave now!"

Jon quickly climbed back into the driver's seat and sped away hoping he would have no further encounters, glad he had thought to fill up the empty spaces in the van after he had loaded the weapons, with furniture and boxes so he could claim he was moving. He still had eight hours of driving and even though he had already driven seven hours he decided to push on and finish the trip today. As the sun was setting, he made it to Piney Flats, Tennessee and stopped at a local restaurant to grab a bite to eat and rest a few minutes. He left after dinner heading north into Virginia to highway 58, traveling east into Hillsville and then headed north up Rt221 until he came to an entrance to the Blue Ridge Parkway and continued north on the parkway past Roanoke then stopped at 1a.m. to make a phone call. He hated to call Clay, but he needed his help.

When Clay answered, Jon said, "It's Jon, Clay, don't say anything, just listen. I need you to bring the wagon to the old entrance on the road. I'll meet you in about 30 minutes."

"Understood," Clay replied and hung up.

Jon tossed the phone into the forest and continued on his journey. In about 30 minutes he was turning onto the backroad which would lead him to the original road to the bunker. He turned off the headlights, keeping the running lights on, looking for the lantern Clay would have burning. He drove slowly, keeping close to the edge of the road and was pleased when he saw the faint glow of the lantern through the trees. As he slowed the van to a stop, he noticed both Clay and Katie waiting for him. He jumped from the truck saying, "We need to hurry."

They quickly unloaded the household boxes and furniture, placing the weapons and ammo into the wagon then repacked the van. When they had finished Clay handed Jon his cell phone as Jon said, "I'm not leaving any more phones with you Clay because things are getting really bad, and the government is monitoring everything now. I know we'll not be able to contact each other but this is for the best."

"I understand," Clay replied.

Jon hugged Katie. "I can't stay, I'll be back when I finish some business."

Katie pleaded, "Jon, please stay here! Reggie would want you to stay here."

Jon released her and marched back to the truck. "I'll see you later." He waved, climbed into the van, made a u turn and was gone.

Clay grabbed her hand. "Come on, Katie he has to do this."

Katie jerked her hand free from Clay's grasp and stomped toward the wagon declaring vehemently, "Men! You both are so stubborn and bullheaded it makes me furious. Just take me home!"

They had a silent ride back to the bunker and found Thomas waiting for them, in a matter of minutes they had the supplies off loaded and stored in the bunker, the horses back in their stalls and were crawling back in their beds.

Clay heard Katie sniffle and realized she was crying, he wiggled close to her back gently wrapping his arm around her, snuggling close and whispered, "Katie, I love you."

She turned to wrap her arms around him. "I'm so afraid Jon is going to get killed."

Attempting to reassure her, he said, "I know sweetheart, but I think he'll be ok, he's smart and tough."

"I hope so." She sobbed.

Clay held her until she fell asleep wishing he was with Jon. He was worried about him. He saw an anger burning in his eyes he had never seen in Iraq, and anger was dangerous, it made you sloppy. He lifted a silent plea to God for Jon's safe return.

CHAPTER 29

The next morning Jon found a landfill and emptied the truck, then returned it to the rental company and was pleased he was in time to catch the next flight out of Roanoke to Las Vegas via Atlanta. As he sat crammed into the tiny commuter plane with about 50 other passenger's he missed the comfort of his father's private jet. It was gone now, destroyed at the Seattle airport and the need to keep his family hidden from the evil in this world meant he could not even submit an insurance claim. His life was changing incredibly fast, and he had no idea where it was heading, but he only had one obsession at the moment. Vengeance. Then he could return to his family.

He was shocked at the difference a week had made at the airport. Armed soldiers stood at every entrance to the facility as police with K-9 drug detectors sniffed every single piece of luggage that passed by them on the baggage carousel or was being brought in by passengers. He felt concern when he realized those leaving the plane had to now show their ID's. He hoped his name had not been added to any terrorist watch lists. As he drew closer to the check point, he felt a shiver ripple over him as a bead of sweat rolled down his spine. Finally, it was his turn, and he placed his driver's license in the police officer's hand who did a quick search on the computer looking for Jon's name. The officer glanced up at Jon, intently gazing at him and it took all of Jon's control to act unconcerned.

He surprised Jon when he asked, "You here to win some money?"

"What?" Jon asked taken aback.

"I see you came in from Virginia and thought you came here to try your luck at the casinos," the officer said gazing inquisitively at Jon.

"Oh. Yeah. I'm sorry, I was thinking about my girlfriend who is coming in later tonight," Jon replied, amazed at how easy lying seemed to be becoming.

The officer chuckled. "Yeah, that'll distract you," He winked at Jon. "Have a nice stay in Vegas!" and he signaled he was free to go.

Jon rushed past him feeling relief wash over him. He was pleased he had no problem getting a taxi and was glad to be back at the hotel. He had not slept in 36 hours and when he lay on the bed to just rest a few minutes he passed out for twelve hours.

A nightmare woke him, and he sat up temporarily confused by his surroundings. He ran his hand through his now shoulder length hair, gazed around the room and remembered he was in Vegas. He was hungry! Wondering what time it was, he glanced at his phone and was shocked to realize it was 10 a.m.

He jumped when a knock sounded at the door and a voice said loudly, "Housekeeping!"

"Not today!" Jon yelled back as he headed to the bathroom. Splashing water in his face, he grabbed a towel to wipe it dry and thought, he would give just about anything for one of Carlitta's omelets. Remembering he was in Vegas, he dressed quickly, and headed down to the first floor to get something decent to eat. He found a restaurant with a breakfast buffet and over did it, but two weeks of fruit and fast food had made him feel empty. After satisfying his hunger, he wandered back to his room and reluctantly picked up his laptop knowing he must once again search the dark web to make plans to get rid of Nimrod. He started his search seeking adult women. He couldn't handle trying to deal with the teen girls. He thought of Nicole and desperately wished he could rescue them all, but that just wasn't possible.

As he was searching, he received notification of an email. Checking the email he was surprised to see it was from Agamemnon. Reluctantly Jon replied, typing "Yes?" "Call me!" Agamemnon demanded. Jon sent his new phone number to Agamemnon and waited.

His phone rang and he answered, "Jon here."

"How are things going?"

"No problems." Jon had no desire to engage in a conversation with Agamemnon.

"Nimrod is still in business."

"Yeah. So?" Jon replied with a hint of impatience.

"Do you need help?"

"No. I had personal business to take care of."

"Yes, I heard about the trouble with your father's company."

Jon felt a shiver slither up his spine. Did this man know everything? Jon made no comment.

Agamemnon continued. "I want you to go to the Roadhouse Motel and knock on door 25."

"Why?"

"Let's just say I have a gift for you."

"What if I'm not interested?"

"Just go, Jon. Be there in an hour."

He hung up before Jon could reply. Jon laid the phone on the bedside table, wondering what he should do. Commonsense told him to run, but curiosity was driving him crazy. He didn't trust Agamemnon at all but decided he would rent a different car and buzz by the motel to see if he could find out what games Agamemnon was playing.

Once he had the new rental car he drove to the motel and was pleased to see there was another motel across the street. Pulling into the parking lot, he parked under a tree and proceeded to watch the Roadhouse Motel. Not wanting to draw attention to himself, Jon turned the engine off, rolled the windows down and preceded to cook in the oppressive desert heat. Several patrons left the motel and with fifteen minutes left in the hour, a beat-up truck pulled into the parking lot in front of room 25 and Jon watched a long-legged blond-haired woman enter the room slamming the door shut. Jon waited another 30 minutes and when nothing happened, he decided he would walk across the street to the front desk of the Roadhouse Motel.

As he walked past the office of the motel where he had his car parked, a skinny pockmarked faced young man came running toward him yelling, "Where ya going? You can't leave that car parked here!"

Jon kept walking, saying menacingly, "Call the police if you want to, but I'll probably be back before they get here."

The man sputtered some more and when Jon continued walking across the street ignoring him, he returned to the office, with no intention of getting the police involved. If he wasn't so fearful of the big man, he would go cut his tires but commonsense prevailed and he plopped himself in front of a TV and ignored what was happening outside.

Jon walked past the front desk and headed toward room 25 on high alert, watching for anything or anyone that appeared out of place.

Satisfied it was safe he knocked on the door. The woman he had seen enter the room, opened the door and asked, "Jon?"

"Yes," Jon replied and carefully entered the room drawing his gun.

The woman panicked. "Hey! What are you doing?" she nearly shouted as Jon grabbed her by the arm, pulling her in front of himself, forcing her toward the bathroom, making sure it was clear, then let her go.

"You're a jerk!" she declared.

"I don't know you and I had to make sure you are alone."

"All you had to do was ask."

"All you had to do was lie," Jon snapped back. "What do you want with me?"

"I'm...here to help you get Nimrod."

Jon's eye's narrowed, shooting daggers, making the woman even more nervous. "What're you talking about?" he asked with a voice as hard as cold steel.

She swallowed hard. Jon glaring at her with his intense blue eyes scared her almost as much as Nimrod. She forced herself to say, "He kidnapped me about a year ago. I hate him! Today, my pimp told me a man called the brothel, and had me delivered to this motel room, paying to have me the whole day." She paused, wringing her hands nervously. "This is terrifying me. When I got to this room, a man calling himself Agamemnon called me and said he only needed me to help his friend get into the brothel to find Nimrod."

"Is Nimrod there?"

"He was when I left this morning. He heard a rumor about Seattle and came back to Vegas right before the bomb went off."

Jon wasn't surprised Nimrod had known about the bomb, if the truth was known, he had probably been the one to arrange the whole thing.

"Why should I trust you?"

She shrugged. "I guess you really don't have any reason to trust me." She glanced up at him, tears shimmering in her gray eyes. "Except Agamemnon told me how you rescued Trixie. I knew her. Can you rescue me?"

Jon felt like he had been gut-punched. He had not anticipated this new twist in his life. A spark of resentment flared toward Agamemnon for giving this girl the hope that he could save her. How many more people would he need to save? He just couldn't say no. Reluctantly he said, "I'll try to rescue you but first I need a name."

She replied, her voice quivering with unshed tears. "Thank you! My name is Tina."

"Ok Tina, how do you plan on helping me get to Nimrod?"

She glanced at him with shocked disbelief. "I don't have any ideas. I thought you had plans."

He shook his head completely frustrated, and started to pace back and forth, while Tina watched him with concern. Suddenly he stopped, turning to face her. "So, I guess I need to get some information."

"Ok.," she replied softly.

"Did you come from the brothel near the racetrack?"

"Yes."

"I'm guessing there is surveillance all over the property and inside."

"Yes. Even in the bedrooms and bathrooms."

"Do you know which room is Nimrod's private room?"

He watched her glance at her feet, and after a few seconds she whispered, "Yes, I know which room is his. I'm one of his favorites, that he enjoys torturing."

"What do you mean torturing?"

"He hates women, and he likes to torture us." She paused gasping for breath, sobs racking her body, as she fought a rising panic attack. "He is evil and does horrible things."

Jon finally touched her, gently holding her hand, understanding her symptoms, and said, "It's ok. I'm here."

Remembering some of the photos he had been unfortunate enough to see, Jon felt sorry for the woman standing before him as anger over the situation burned in his soul. He must stop this monster.

"Is there any way I can get into the brothel without renting a girl? Do you ever have advanced notice of when he is going to call you?"

"No, not usually. One of the pimps comes and gets us when we are requested."

"I need time to make plans. Will he let you come back to this motel if I pay for a full day?"

"Yes," she whispered despondently when she realized he was going to send her back to the brothel.

Jon wanted to comfort her but knew he could not, he needed her to go back. "I'm sorry, Tina, but right now you are my only hope. I promise to save you if you can help me. We just can't run away without a plan. He'll find us if we do." He looked at her, his blue eyes begging her to understand.

She sighed. "OK. I'll help."

"Thanks. I'll be in touch." And he left the room, leaving her alone and crying.

He walked back across the street, sat back in his car, and again watched. He watched as Tina cautiously stepped out of the room and looked around. She reminded Jon of a skittish colt ready to bolt at the first sign of danger. She turned to reenter the room and when the same truck which had dropped her off pulled back into the parking lot she climbed in, and the truck drove away. Jon watched a while longer then returned to the Bellagio.

Jon desperately wanted to help Tina and eliminate Nimrod. Ideas eluded him. How was he going to get near him without entering the brothel? And keep Agamemnon out of it?

Over the next few days, he ate very little and slept even less. His dilemma was gnawing at him. He drove around Vegas and even played a few slot machines trying to ease his tortured mind, without success. He needed to get rid of Nimrod. Out of desperation he called the brothel and requested Tina be delivered to the Roadhouse motel room 25 and paid the ridiculous price. He once again parked a different rental car in a different motel parking lot and walked to the Roadhouse. He sat in the lobby, telling the suspicious clerk he was waiting for a friend, and watched. The same beat up truck dropped her off and he continued to wait. After about 30 minutes he decided it was safe and wandered to room 25 and knocked on the door. Tina peeked out and then opened the door wide when she saw it was him.

Jon entered the room saying, "Hi. I need to talk."

He took a good look at her and noticed the dark circles under her eyes and the bruises on her arms. She didn't look well. "Are you feeling ok?"

She shrugged. "Yeah, I'm ok. Just been a rough couple of days. What do you need?"

"Are you hungry? I can order delivery for us," Jon asked.

"Thanks, but I'm fine."

She sat down on the bed, and he sat in the only chair in the room. "I'm having difficulty making plans to get Nimrod. So, I thought I would ask some more questions."

"I'll try my best to help."

CHAPTER 30

Nimrod was wondering why Tina had been called out of the brothel for a private rendezvous two times in one week and he had followed her to the motel and now sat in the same parking lot Jon had sat in the first time Agamemnon had sent him there. He had watched a man leave the motel office and walk to the room and Tina let him enter. So, she knew him. Something fishy was going on. Two hours later as he watched the stranger leave the room and walk up the street, he had a vague flash of memory. He felt he knew the man but no matter how hard he tried to retrieve the memory, it stayed buried out of reach. Frustration made him angry. He instructed his bodyguard, who was driving, to discreetly follow Jon.

Jon felt the hair on his neck prickle, wondering what the danger was. He slowed and looked around noticing a dark SUV, which rolled past him. He watched the SUV and then made another sweep of the area and not seeing anything, hurried to his waiting car.

When Jon slowed and watched the SUV Nimrod was riding in, drive past him, Nimrod realized in shock he did know who he was, the long hair and beard didn't fool him, he would recognize Jon Sadler anywhere and a violent rage erupted in his soul. He must arrange a meeting with him. He would finally kill Jon.

After talking with Tina, Jon realized his chances of getting into the brothel undetected were slim. It was well guarded and protected.

Two days later he was shocked when Tina called him whispering, "Jon, please meet me at the motel. I have a plan."

Jon ignored the warnings screaming in his head and headed to the hotel. Knocking on the door of room 25 yet again, he slipped inside when Tina opened it. He immediately noticed Tina was acting extremely nervous, glancing around the room and not saying a word he walked alertly toward the bathroom. Suddenly a large man jumped in front of him, making Tina scream in terror. He attempted to punch Jon, who jumped back out of reach, and bumped into Tina flipping backward over the chair. When Jon jumped to his feet, his skull met the hard handle of the attacker's handgun which caused him to crumple to the floor. The man dragged Jon's limp body out to a waiting car, and shoving him into the car, he ordered Tina into the backseat with Jon. They headed north on interstate 15 driving into the desert.

Jon moaned as Tina gently brushed his hair away from his scalp and noticed a small trickle of blood. She hated that she had been used to lure Jon into this, knowing Nimrod must plan on killing him, the further they drove into the desert. Tina noticed Jon was awake and pretending to be unconscious, he signaled her to remain quiet. The driver slowed the car and Jon carefully removed his handgun from the holster under his left arm and held it by his side, surprising Tina, who realized the man driving had been sloppy when checking Jon for weapons and missed the small 38 revolver he had tucked under his arm. When the driver stopped the car, he made a quick glance into the back seat and assuming Jon was still unconscious he jumped from the car and opened the back door. Tina screamed, covering her ears when the air exploded with the gun shot that sent Jon's abductor flying backwards. Tina flung her door open and tried to run away when suddenly she was grabbed by the arm and turning, saw to her horror that Nimrod gripped her arm. Jon scrambled from the car and knelt behind the vehicle trying to assess his options.

He saw a man grab Tina and pull her close to himself using her as a shield, as Tina screamed, "Nimrod, let me go!"

Nimrod was here! Jon fought the urge to run toward them to confront him. "Jon, come out!"

Jon was shocked, he recognized that voice, but where had he heard it? Jon heard the door to the crumbling gas station burst open and swung around shooting the man who exited the building, raising his semi-automatic rifle toward Jon, and quickly swung back around searching for the man holding Tina. He couldn't find them.

"Over here," said that familiar voice. It was driving Jon crazy; he just couldn't place the voice with the face.

He glanced toward the direction of the voice to find them standing beside a limo. Jon stood up and faced the man. "Let her go!" he demanded.

Nimrod laughed. "Come here."

Jon stood glued to the spot gazing at the stranger with the familiar voice. He had no intention of going anywhere near the man.

"I will kill her if you do not come here."

Jon watched as Tina shivered and started to cry. "Please don't kill me."

The man threw her to the ground in front of him laughing. "Beg some more."

Tina sat up brushing the dirt and gravel from her bleeding knees and glanced at Jon with pleading eyes. Jon couldn't resist that look. He had to help her. He walked toward them slowly and tossed his pistol to the ground when directed by Nimrod. As he drew close to Tina, he stretched forth his hand to help her up when a shot rang out and she crumpled to the ground holding her stomach. Jon moved so fast it startled Nimrod, who didn't have time to react. Jon punched him in the jaw, sending him toppling backward, then Jon jumped on top of him and pummeled him about the head and face until Nimrod passed out.

He ran back to Tina, lifting her head. "Tina?" he whispered.

She glanced at him with dull pain-filled eyes. "Jon...I could've loved a man like you."

His heart constricted with pain as he held her close. "I'm sorry, Tina. I didn't save you."

She never heard him as her head slumped to the side and Jon realized she was dead. Rage burned in his soul making his stomach churn. He had much to make Nimrod pay for. He glanced at the man lying on the ground and when he moaned Jon kicked him in the head and side making sure he was still unconscious and went looking for something to tie him up with; finding a rope, he returned to tie him. He had enough to tie his wrists, and when he was done, he placed him in the back seat of the limo. Slamming the door, he crawled into the front seat and making sure the dividing window was raised he started his journey.

He drove back toward Vegas heading toward the brothel because he knew there were some abandoned warehouses near there. He cautiously pulled the car in behind a building and locking Nimrod in the car he went to do a quick search of the building. He found a small office in the interior of the empty building with no windows, a beat-up office chair and to his amazement he found a bag of large zip ties sitting on one of the work benches, grabbing them he made his way back to the car to find Nimrod laying on the ground beside the car, hands still tied behind his back, desperately trying to get his hands loose.

Jon walked up to him and stopped just out of his reach. Nimrod glanced up at him and recognition hit Jon like a ton of bricks. "You are Nimrod?" Jon asked incredulously.

The man growled, "Yes." Hatred burning in his eyes.

Jon walked up to him and kicked at one of his legs and Nimrod grunted when the prosthetic leg sailed free of his body, banging to a stop against a wall. Jon kicked the other leg free of Nimrod's body, then pulled him into the room in the warehouse, as Nimrod cursed and yelled while Jon zip tied his wrists tightly to the chair and used an appliance cord he had found to tie Nimrod's body around his waist to the office chair and closing the door, he shoved a screw driver through the lock latch, then moved a heavy work bench in front of the door so it could not be opened from the inside and left.

Jon returned to the motel and left the limo in the parking lot, then drove his own rental car to an outdoorsman store and purchased a large hunting knife, then drove back to the warehouse and was pleased to find no evidence that anybody was here. He entered the warehouse and stopped to listen. Nimrod was yelling for someone to let him loose. Good, he was still tied to the chair.

After Jon determined it was safe, he entered the office room, glancing at the man he had tied to the chair. He still could not get over his shock. He asked again, anger raging in his soul, "So you are Nimrod?"

The man grinned venomously up at Jon. "Surprised ain't ya?"

"Why, Austin? Why did you do this?"

It seemed like the face of the man once known as Sergeant Austin, contorted into a grotesque vile visage, eyes burning with an evil so intense Jon was startled.

"You are responsible for this," Austin growled gesturing with his head toward his missing legs. "You took my legs and manhood from me!" he hissed.

"Me?" Jon said in disbelief. "How did I take your legs from you?"

"You led us down that street in Iraq right into an ambush. I have lived for the day I could get even with you! Lived for the day I could make you suffer as I have suffered!" Austin paused then rushed on with great excitement at the pain he was about to inflict on the man who enflamed his consuming rage. "The best day of my life was when I crushed every bone inch by inch in your little brother's legs. I wasn't going to kill him, just cripple him for life, like you did me, but when your father refused to pay the ransom...well... I just got carried away...and we know the outcome."

Austin watched Jon slowly walk toward him as he pulled the large razor-sharp hunting knife from its sheath, "You ain't got it in you, little rich boy," Austin jeered with a hatred born of Satan.

Jon stopped in front of him, and ripped Nimrod's shirt open which caused him to laugh. Pausing, Jon said coldly, "You know, I was the one who took Trixie from you. She belongs to me now."

Nimrod gazed at him in disbelief, then roared like a caged animal when he saw the truth in Jon's eyes. Struggling to free himself, he fell over striking his head on the cement floor knocking himself unconscious. Jon pushed him back to an upright position.

When Nimrod regained consciousness, Jon took the knife and cut slowly from Austin's navel up to his sternum cutting about an inch deep as Austin bit his lip trying not to make a sound. Jon watched the blood start to flow down his torso with great enjoyment.

"Tell me, Austin, while I do this, how much you enjoy your slow death."

"Never!" he sneered at Jon.

Jon then cut across his abdomen from under his right rib toward the left rib. A sharp gasp escaped Austin's lips as Jon laughed. "Did that hurt?"

Jon sat down across from Austin saying, "I think you need a rest. Do you?"

Austin glanced up at him, hatred gleaming in his eyes. He did not answer because the pain was so intense, he could not speak.

"Well, I think we'll sit here and watch your blood decorate the floor," Jon stated sarcastically.

After few minutes Austin's head dropped down toward his chest and Jon shook him. "Wake up! You don't want to miss the finale.'"

Austin turned his face up to look at Jon, the pain now showing through the anger. He screamed when Jon slowly stabbed the knife all the way to the hilt into his abdomen. Next Jon pulled it back out just as slowly feeling deep satisfaction when he screamed again. He was going to scream until he died to pay for every torturous scream Jon knew Reggie had made when he was being killed. Jon jabbed and sliced as the screams and groans grew weaker then stepped back when the last cut did not bring a response, grabbing a handful of Austin's hair, he pulled his head back so he could look into his face. A feeling of great joy and relief washed over him when he realized he had succeeded. Those who had murdered Reggie were dead and now he could go home. He turned and walked away from Nimrod with the mistaken thought that now that he had completed his quest for vengeance, he would find solace.

As Jon exited the warehouse he stopped abruptly when Agamemnon stepped in front of him. Jon had not realized he had followed him and most likely had watched the whole encounter. His blood ran cold when Agamemnon gazed at him with hard cold eyes.

"I'm finished with you now, Jon. Well done. Nimrod will no longer irritate me." Agamemnon's lips twitched into a reluctant grin when he saw the realization and horror cross Jon's face. "Yes, I helped you and I used you."

He reached out one of those huge hands and gripped Jon on the shoulder. Jon refused to give him the satisfaction of showing any pain. Agamemnon continued. "I usually kill anyone who finishes a job for me, that I can no longer use, but I can't kill you, Jon...because of Iraq. Go Jon, and don't ever let me see you again or you...will...die."

Jon watched in stunned silence as the man whom he had thought was a friend turned his back on him and entered a waiting SUV. Jon climbed into his jeep after Agamemnon left and drove to a parking garage two hours away, parked the jeep in the first empty slot he could find, grabbed his overnight bag and left. He could no longer drive it as the GPS and tracking systems built into each new car would allow him to be followed by whomever took the initiative to follow him. He walked another two miles to a local mall and was pleased to see the 1980 gray sedan he had parked there two days ago, still there. The old car had no computer systems, making it impossible to track, but someone could have placed a tracking device on the car recently, so he took out his electronic scanner which would pick up any tracking or GPS devices and once he had determined the car was clean, he opened the door and began his cross-country journey.

REDEMPTION

CHAPTER 31

Jon arrived in Roanoke a week later and once again enlisted Fred's help to get to the bunker. He silently entered the main living area and cringed when the family joyfully rushed him. He wanted to be left alone.

Betty stopped and gazed at her son, disturbed by the blank look in his eyes. She placed her hand on his arm asking, "Jon, are you feeling ok?"

He focused on her, forcing a smile while the rest of the family was quieted by Jon's actions. He was scaring Nicole. "I'm fine, Mom. Just tired. I'm going to grab a bite to eat, shower and take a nap."

They watched him sit at the table as Nicole wandered over and sat down across from him. "Jon?" she asked softly.

He glanced at her, emotionless, saying, "Yes?"

"I missed you." She smiled weakly, overcome with concern for him.

"You are safe now, Nicole."

She answered him, "I am?"

"Yes, sweetheart. They will never look for you again." he replied, his vacant eyes as cold as ice.

He took the last bite of his snack and stood up walking to the family hall saying nothing. Amos watching him was worried. His son was suffering, fighting his demons and Amos didn't know how to help.

He glanced at Betty when she asked through her tears, "What is wrong with him, Amos?"

Amos went to her and held her reassuringly. "I think he has been through much, Betty. We need to give him a chance to deal with everything."

"I'm worried about him."

"I know, honey. So am I."

They did not see him until the next morning when he strode into the living room declaring, "I'll be back."

"But, Jon, where are you going?" Katie asked fearfully.

"Just going riding. I'll be back later."

Nicole rushed after him. "Can I please go?"

He replied harshly, "I want to be alone."

They all watched him rush from the room as Katie wrapped her arms around a crying Nicole.

"What is wrong?" she asked breathlessly.

"I don't know," whispered Katie.

Nicole moved away from Katie, and they watched as she silently sat down on the couch. Betty watching her thought, the child desperately needed Jon, but Betty didn't think he was capable of helping her at the moment. Whatever had happened in his life must be bad, he had never been this way when he returned home from fighting in Iraq.

Suddenly, Nicole took off running after Jon, with Clay and Katie chasing after her. All three of them entered the stable at the same time, Jon turning to glare at them. He swung himself into the saddle and paused, saying, "Don't follow me! I want to be alone."

"But, Jon, please," Nicole pleaded through bitter tears.

"No!" he declared angrily kicking the horse into action. Once outside he pushed the horse into a gallop, following the large creek away from the bunker.

Nicole ran toward the other stall and flinging the stall gate open she attempted to grab the horse's halter just as Katie grabbed her hand. "No, Nicole!"

Nicole turned eyes burning with fear and anger toward Katie and Clay. "You have no right to stop me!"

Katie said calmly, "Yes I do, Nicole."

"NO, YOU DON'T!" she screamed trying to force her way past Katie as the horse reared his head back, pulling free from her grasp.

"STOP IT!" Clay roared, startling both women who turned to gaze at him in stunned silence. "I was with Jon in Iraq, and I know him pretty good. We'll leave him alone."

Clay watched the anger creep back into Nicole's eyes. "If you fight me on this, Nicole. I will lock you in your room."

Nicole, saving Clay the effort, ran back up to the main floor and locked herself in her bedroom. She only wanted to help Jon just like he had helped her. Who made Clay the one in charge anyway?

Jon pushed the horse hard wanting to escape. He pulled the horse to a stop at the ridge top when he left the meadow and gazed in silence at the valleys and mountains rolling away to the western horizon, not noticing anything, lost in his thoughts. The nightmares were much worse than those he had suffered after coming back from Iraq, the memories of the war now mingled with the memories of his revenge, and he was having serious thoughts about just ending it all. It would be so easy. Just pull the trigger and be done with the pain and heartbreak. In many ways he felt like such a failure.

Reluctantly, he turned the horse around and rode at a leisurely pace back to the bunker. He knew he couldn't hurt his parents by taking his own life. He knew nothing about the Tribulation but thought if what was going on in the world now was any indication of how bad it was going to be, he needed to protect his family.

Once back inside the bunker he unsaddled the horse and when he had finished caring for the animal, he slowly made his way back upstairs, dreading encountering his family. He needed to be alone. He just couldn't handle all the happy emotions when he was in torment.

He was relieved when Clay walked up to him as he entered the living area and said, "I've got the laptop turned on and secure from prying eyes so we can go over a few things."

Jon followed him to the office space in the corner across from the kitchen and sat down beside Clay as they began going over the figures of how much fuel and energy was being used and the list of supplies consumed and the inventory remaining. This occupied his mind for a couple of hours, until they were called to lunch. Jon sat at the table picking at his lunch as he silently watched and listened to the banter of his family. He was glad to see Thomas and Nicole seemed to be adjusting well to being with his family, Nicole had gained some weight and the haunted look was gone from her eyes. He was happy he had been able to save her, but Tina's pleading eyes flashed in his memory sending him into his familiar feelings of failure at his inability to save her, and Reggie. He quietly got up making his way to his room. The family stopped talking and watched him walk away, sadness and despair settling on them, as no one knew how to help him.

The weeks stretched into months as Jon sank deeper into his depression. His family desperately prayed and attempted to engage him in their daily activities, but he staunchly refused to join in. Most days he rose early and taking one of the horses he would leave to spend time making sure the property was secure, which it always was. Once he made it all the way to the little restaurant at the entrance to the trail and planned on stopping for lunch but was disappointed to find it had closed.

He tried to contact Fred but without success, his phone was no longer in service and Jon wondered how he was doing and hoped his family was safe.

Nicole attempted to go with him several times but finally gave up when he angrily refused to let her join him. He had saved her, and she couldn't help him. She desperately wanted to help him. She was thankful for Jon's sisters, especially Katie who was only eight years older than she. They seemed to have similar thoughts about the same things, and she had finally shared with Katie what had happened to her and where Jon had found her, relieved when Katie did not judge her.

CHAPTER 32

Jon sat down on his bed leaning his head into his hands as the darkness engulfed him again, the anger and bitterness raging inside of him consumed his every thought, even his dreams, a darkness so deep he was beginning to think he would never be able to crawl back to the light. He had found his revenge but at what cost to himself, he had no peace and solace eluded him. He felt like he was in a long tunnel and the light had become a tiny speck very far away which seemed to grow dimmer every day. How was he going to make it back? How was he going to change from monster back to human? Chloe had been talking to him about Jesus. She had told him that Jesus was the only one who could help him. The only one who could ease his tortured soul. At one time, a long time ago it seemed, he had wondered if there was a God, but after what had happened and the thing's he had done, he thought even if there was a God, He couldn't save him.

A knock sounded on his bedroom door, and he bid Chloe enter when she softly called his name. She gently sat on the bed beside him, not speaking. He finally glanced up at her and it broke her heart to see the agony in his beautiful blue eyes.

"Jon, I love you," she whispered.

He didn't know how to respond. How could anyone ever love him again?

"I'll listen if you ever need to talk." She paused, then continued, realizing he might lash out at her, but she had to tell him. "Jon, God knows what you are going through. He cares for you even more than I do."

She was amazed when there was no anger, only anguish. "God could never forgive or love me!"

"He loves you so much He let Jesus die for you," Chloe pleaded.

She wanted to hold him but wisely knew he would pull away, so she stood up. "I love you and will always listen."

When she reached to open the door, she heard the most agonizing sound she had ever heard when Jon pleaded, "Help me, Chloe. Help me accept God's forgiveness!"

She rushed back to him and kneeling in front of him she started to pray. "Please, God help Jon to ask You for forgiveness and accept Your gift of salvation through Your Son Jesus."

Then to her amazement she listened to her brother's heartbreaking plea. "Oh God, Chloe says You can love me and forgive me. I'm not sure You can. Help me, God! Please help me! I'm so sorry for the horrible things I have done." He paused trying to gulp air into his lungs as he cried bitter tears. "Please forgive me. Please save me. I believe in Jesus."

Then he bent his head down as his body was racked with gut wrenching sobs. Sitting back on the bed next to Jon, Chloe gently placed her arm around his shoulders and just sat quietly beside him. He finally glanced at her and whispered, "Has God saved me, Chloe?"

"Yes, He has, Jon." She paused. "Now God wants you to forgive yourself. Whatever has happened in your life is in the past and God will help you to forgive yourself." She smiled and glanced around conspiratorially. "Dad even asked God for forgiveness," she whispered.

Jon said in disbelief, "Dad did?"

She replied softly, "Yes, he did, Jon, and I know Reggie is in heaven shouting for joy that we are all saved. He told me, the day before the kidnapping he had accepted Jesus as his Savior. So, Jon, we will see him again soon."

Fresh tears slid down Jon's cheeks. "Thank you for sharing that, Chloe."

Chloe stood up. "Come on, Jon, let's go tell Mom and Dad."

Jon stood up, dreading the encounter with his father as he followed Chloe into the family room and found his parents sitting together on one of the sofas talking quietly. Might as well get it over with, Jon thought, as he walked toward his parents.

Chloe declared excitedly, "Jon needs to tell you something."

Betty glanced up at her son with anticipation, but Amos felt dread settle on him. He knew things about Jon, that Jon was not aware he knew. He lifted a silent plea toward heaven hoping Jon would not decide he needed to confess his sins to them. Amos knew Betty would not fully understand the rage that had driven Jon, but Amos understood completely. He was ashamed to admit to himself, but he had even been thrilled that Jon had sought out the revenge he could not.

Jon declared hastily, "I've accepted Jesus as my Savior."

Betty jumped up, throwing her arms around her son. "Oh, Jon, I'm so happy!"

Jon hugged his mother tightly, thrilled she was happy for him. She stepped away from him when Amos was finally on his feet and Jon was astonished when his father wrapped his arms around him also. For the first time in his life, that he could remember, his father was hugging him. He fought the urge to pull away and demand a comfortable distance between them. Instead, reaching down, he hugged his father back. They held each other for a few moments, relief and forgiveness washing over Jon. In that instant Jon realized his father did love him, and the light at the end of that dark tunnel suddenly burned brighter and Jon felt hope for the first time since his burning rage had sent him down the path of his vengeance.